THE EAGLE

THE EAGLE

JILLIAN DODD

Jillian Dodd Inc.
N. Redington Beach, FL

ISBN: 978-1-940652-93-1

THIS BOOK IS DEDICATED TO ALL THE
WRITERS WHO SPARKED MY
IMAGINATION AS A CHILD AND MADE
ME DREAM OF BEING A SPY SOMEDAY.

And to the people who

humored me.

BOOKS BY JILLIAN DODD

If you tell a lie loud enough and long enough, people will believe it.
-Adolph Hitler

PROLOGUE

TWO MEN ARE seated in a large room with ornate gold leaf bookcases and a deeply toned, hand-painted mural covering a large, domed ceiling. The mural features the Archangel Michael in a battle with Satan. It was painstakingly created for this room based on the Baroque painting, "The Fall of the Damned," and it took an artist three years to complete.

Although one of the men seated owns the home this beautiful room is in, he is not sitting in a place of power behind his mammoth hand-carved mahogany desk, but rather both men are seated in matching wingback chairs covered in the softest of plaid cashmeres and are situated near the room's French doors, which overlook the estate's vast grounds.

"We have some loose ends to tie up regarding

Montrovia," the owner of the home says after taking a sip of amber-colored liquid from a heavy crystal tumbler.

"We shouldn't have trusted the girl," the other man says.

"Easy to say in retrospect, especially considering she came very close to succeeding. If she would have become Queen, it would have made things much easier for us. We will prevail, regardless."

"What is our next course of action, then?"

"We continue with our plan," the owner states. "Although, I'm afraid there will have to be a few slight variations."

"Does one of those variations have to do with why the Eagle wasn't present at our meeting today?" the man asks, the understanding of an unusual event earlier in the day showing in his furrowed brow.

"He isn't doing what he promised. Now that he controls the world's most powerful military, he seems to have forgotten who put him into power."

"That *was* a very expensive endeavor."

The owner of the home nods in agreement. "One of which we are not reaping the reward from. So, I'm afraid we have no choice. We must liquidate our bad investment."

The man sets his drink down, trying to keep his hand from shaking, knowing it could just as easily be him if he dared to cross the man in front of him. "But he's our friend."

"Something he has also forgotten. Do it. And I only want the best, for obvious reasons."

"Sadly, the best is dead."

"Are you referring to The Priest?"

"Yes. He was killed after the Eagle's father hired him for a hit then double crossed him."

"I don't believe he's dead. Find him."

"I'm sure we can find someone equally as talented—"

"I want The Priest and *no one* else," the owner interrupts.

How in the world am I supposed to hire a dead man? he thinks, but he doesn't dare say.

"It's going to be dangerous for us to even *try* to find him, but I will see what I can come up with. What if he is still alive, but says no?"

"You will make him an offer he cannot refuse. And see if he will give us a group discount regarding the outstanding Montrovian situation."

THE ASSASSIN KNOWN as The Priest enters an empty bar in France. The hole-in-the-wall drinking establishment is supposed to be open this afternoon, but the owner just hung the closed sign on the door.

"What is this nonsense about an offer?" the assassin asks, freaking out a little. "Everyone thinks I'm dead. We've worked hard to establish ourselves here. How did they contact you?"

"Through a secure network. I left a few trusted assets in place in case we ever needed the money."

"We could be traced though that."

"No, we can't. I'm good at what I do. Are you interested in hearing the offer, or not?"

"It doesn't matter how much it is. I'm not interested."

"So are you saying that fifteen million dollars wouldn't sway you?"

"Fifteen million? Who the hell is the target?"

"It's a series of three hits, but they have only revealed the first one." He whispers the man's name.

"You've got to be kidding. No way."

"This money could set us both up for life."

"We're already set up for life. Sort of. Besides, I retired. With good reason."

"They will go as high as twenty."

"You know how well-guarded a man of his stature is."

"Are you saying no because you don't want to do it, or because you don't think you can do it?"

"Whether or not I can do it is not the question. I always complete my tasks. However, in this case, getting away with it would be another story. I'd have a whole country after me. And they'd find you first, since you are the one brokering the deal."

"You don't trust my skills?"

"All I know is that I'm lucky to be alive. It's been over six years since I was double-crossed, and you know as well as I do, that when Lara was killed it should have been me driving. I had gotten careless with my cover."

"That was four years ago."

"Two years after I was presumed dead. Men like that never forget. For all we know, this could be their way of setting me up." He pushes himself away from the bar. "No. We can't risk it."

"If we could get them to twenty-five million, we could buy our own island and live in paradise forever."

"We already live in paradise, my friend."

"I'm tired of running this bar."

"This bar is your cover. Hiding didn't work before. Hiding in plain sight is. And we will continue to make it work."

"Whatever," the bartender says, his disappointment showing in both his expression and gestures. But he does as told—logs into a secure network and declines the offer.

He's surprised when there is an immediate response.

"They just offered thirty million."

The assassin closes his eyes. The thrill of the hunt is something he craves, but he can't.

He shakes his head no.

The bartender relays his decision, then his eyes go

wide with shock.

"You need to see this for yourself," he says, handing him the laptop.

The assassin reads the instant message.

Thirty million is my final offer, but I suspect it's not about the money. I have other information that may interest you. The first target is not only a powerful world leader, but he is the legacy of the man who double-crossed you six years ago.

He's rereading it again just to be sure, when another message pops up.

Does that change your mind?

The assassin drains the beer in front of him. "Tell the man that it most certainly does."

MISSION: DAY ONE

My cell buzzes on the table next to me as I'm sunning on the upper deck of the Royal Yacht, fending off a slight hangover and lack of sleep.

I smile when Lorenzo's name pops up on the screen.

"How's Ibiza treating you?" he asks.

"Ibiza is one big party."

"It has quite the club scene. Have you been relaxing, as well?"

"Hard not to on your beautiful boat," I reply, glancing around at the sheer luxury of the place. Amazing how quickly I have become accustomed to it.

"Have you thrown any parties? I'll be honest, I was hoping to get an invite."

"No parties. Daniel is up early training every morning. The Olympic tryouts are a few weeks away, so he hasn't really—"

"Wait. Did you just say that *Daniel* is on my boat? *With you?*"

"Uh, yeah."

"Why?"

"Because you sent him here to be my party?"

"Lee," he says, his voice sounding strained, "you and I—you know how I feel about you."

"And you know how I feel about you."

"Yet you suggested I call Elizabeth," he counters.

"Did you?"

"No, Huntley, I did not." He sighs. "Even though I was upset to learn the truth about you, I'm certainly not over you. And I could *never* offer you up to another man."

A quick glance over the railing confirms that Daniel is still training in the pool a deck below. Knowing I won't be overheard, I say, "I'm sorry, Lorenzo. If I weren't who I am, if I didn't have to do this—"

"Things would be different," he says, finishing my sentence. "I know. I'm a King and you're—you. It would never work."

"Right."

"But what if it could?" he asks.

"The only way it could is if one of us were willing to quit."

"I can't quit my country."

"So you want *me* to quit?"

"I'm not sure. I have so many unanswered questions."

"What were you told about me?"

"Very little. The man who called simply stated that your training and cover had taken years to put into place. He then requested I not tell a soul, for your personal safety."

"Lorenzo, it's one thing to know what I do. It's another thing to have witnessed it."

"While I will admit your talents are slightly unusual, it doesn't make them any less spectacular."

"You saw me kill people. I'm good at it."

"And thank goodness that you are, or I'd be dead."

"And I'm a liar."

"I watched you work the crowd to perfection at both the Queen's Garden Party and Her Majesty's Royal Ball. Where I come from, we call that being diplomatic."

I laugh out loud. "You almost make me feel like a normal girl."

"Will you tell me how you ended up in this profession at such a young age?"

"Can I be honest with you?"

"Of course."

"I'm not doing this for my country."

"Good, then it will be easier to convince you to live in mine."

What he says tugs at my heartstrings, but once he knows everything, I know he won't feel that way. "To answer your question, I ended up in this profession because my parents were spies."

"That was not in your dossier. Were they really killed in a car accident?"

"Lorenzo, what's in my dossier is what they want people to see, and what I'm about to tell you is probably going to make you hate me more."

"I don't hate you, Huntley. I don't think I ever could. I'm sorry I reacted so badly, but there was so much to deal with at once—being kidnapped, discovering I was your mission, my father's passing, and then becoming King. I'm known as the Playboy Prince. Women flock to me. The idea that I was your job was so foreign to me that it's taken a bit to sink in. But I keep coming back to one thing. Do you remember what you said to me after our mermaid bath?"

"That when you drop all the prince shit and be yourself, I really like you."

"Tell me the truth, Huntley. Were those your true feelings?"

"Yes."

"See, I feel the same way. Your job is not what enthralls me about you, *you* do. Not to mention that I will never be able to look at a chess game and not think of—"

"I'm doing it for myself," I interrupt. I can't let him

think we have a chance. Because we don't. In no world can I envision being lucky enough to be with a guy like him. Besides, once I tell him the truth, he'll see me as the hardened assassin I was trained to be.

"Because you like killing people?"

"No, because my mother was murdered in front of me."

He audibly sucks in his breath. "Oh, Lee."

"I managed to shoot and wound the assassin and then escaped."

"How old were you?"

"Twelve. A few days later, my father's car exploded. I got out. He didn't. I was sent to a very private school and trained for this."

"So you seek revenge?"

"Yes. I'm going to find the assassin."

"Then what?"

"Kill him."

"Huntley, revenge won't change anything. It won't bring your mother back."

"It's my fault she's dead. If I had been better trained, I would have killed the assassin before he killed her. I had a gun—I knew how to use it—but I was scared. I'm not scared anymore."

"You were only twelve. It's not your fault. You can't just go kill the man."

"Yes, I can. He deserves to die. You told me it was

okay that I killed the bad guys in order to rescue you. You said they *deserved* to die. That makes you a hypocrite. Killing people is fine when it saves *your* life, is that it?"

"Maybe you are right. How about we agree to disagree?"

"This is why we could never be together, Lorenzo. I was trained to kill bad people. What if an assassin had killed your father? Would you send your army after him? The Montrovian Secret Forces? Would you want revenge?"

"Yes, I probably would," he says with a sigh. "It's just that I wouldn't be the one pulling the trigger."

"And that makes it any better?"

"No, you're right. It doesn't. Lee, I care about you. I worry about you. Look, just promise me, from this moment forward, we will both be completely honest with each other. About what we're doing and about our feelings. Can you agree to that?"

I hesitate. I was trained to lie, but those lies are meant to both protect me and further my mission. Lorenzo already knows the truth about me, so I'm not sure quite how to respond. "I can sort of agree."

"I'm afraid I need more of a commitment than that."

"Some of the things I may be asked to do will have to be kept secret."

"Fine. Then can you at least agree to be honest with

me about your feelings?"

"Yes, that I can do."

"Very well. I hope that means you will be able to handle what I'm about to say."

I brace myself for it. I'm so torn emotionally when it comes to him. Part of me wants to tell him goodbye forever. The other part of me wants to never let him go.

"Daniel's being on my boat does not make me happy. Did you really believe I am so gracious?"

"I will admit, I was surprised, but I assumed it was because you no longer had feelings for me. When you kissed me after the coronation, it felt like goodbye. You gave Ari girls. I thought you gave me Daniel."

"I'm far from over you."

"I'm not sure I will ever be over you," I say, kicking myself the second the words come tumbling out of my mouth.

"But yet you and Daniel have been together."

"Not as much as you would think."

"Anything is too much, and I am typically quite liberal sexually. Was Daniel part of your mission, too?"

"You were my only mission, but we were purposely seated with him and Peter Prescott at a gala. The plan was to befriend both of them in the hope that they would give our cover validity."

"And our encounter at the tailor's shop? That was also somehow set up?"

"Nope. That was completely by chance. I was shocked when you walked in."

"So the fates brought us together regardless of your plan?"

"I guess, maybe."

"You played very coy with me. I was crushed when you didn't come to my party."

"Had I gone, I would have just been another notch on your bedpost."

"Perhaps."

"Definitely." I laugh.

"It feels good to hear you laugh. Now, please go tell Daniel to get the hell off my boat, otherwise I may be forced to have the Captain throw him overboard."

"Be sure they take his trainer, too."

"You are sleeping with him, as well?"

"No, of course not. But since he arrived, I haven't slept with Daniel. His training exhausts him."

"I like the man already. So, when are you coming home?"

"Home?"

"To Montrovia. It is your home now, Contessa Von Allister, and I would very much like you back in my country where I can keep an eye on you. How would you feel about me sending the chopper to pick you up? Rescue you from boredom."

"*You're* going to rescue *me*?" I can't help but laugh,

especially considering I've saved his life on numerous occasions. "Any chance you could wear shining armor, ride in on a horse, give me the full fairytale treatment?"

"If that's what it takes. Although, the Queen's Ball felt like a fairytale to me. Did it not to you?"

"Part of it."

"Which parts?"

"In your office. When I first saw you dressed in full military garb. It was easy to forget you were a prince sometimes. That night, you definitely looked the part. Then there were the shoes. And the dress. And the jewels."

"But not the dance?"

"Not the dance. I had to constantly be vigilant. You were so exposed. I was stupid to take Allie to the restroom. I should have never left you. I screwed up and let my guard down."

"In retrospect, it's a good thing you did. Otherwise, you would have gotten a dart to the neck, and Ari and I would have been shark bait."

I consider this. "Maybe you're right."

"So when we were alone, we felt like a fairytale?"

"In most fairytales, the girl doesn't lie to the Prince."

"Cinderella did."

"She didn't lie. She just omitted a few details about herself."

"Does Daniel know what you do?"

"No."

"Are you going to tell him?"

"I can't."

"Do you love him?"

"I care for him—but I'm not supposed to have feelings for anyone. It was part of my training."

"You can't train people not to love—" The sound of a door banging open causes him to stop mid-sentence.

I hear the voice of his trusted guard, Juan. "Sorry to interrupt, Your Highness, but I thought you would want to know. The President of the United States has just been shot."

"Um, hang on, Huntley." He says to Juan, "Can you repeat that?"

"The President of the United States was shot, possibly fatally. It happened only a few minutes ago."

"Did you hear that?" Lorenzo asks me.

"I did," I say, getting up and slipping into a robe. How could this be? They send me to save the Prince of a teeny country like Montrovia but allow our own President to get shot?

I rush down the stairs to the salon, grab the remote control from the bar, and flip on the television.

And there it is running across the bottom of the screen: *Breaking News: The President of the United States has been shot.*

"I'm turning on CNN," Lorenzo says. The sound on

his end is a few seconds ahead of mine.

An anchorman is discussing law with a White House correspondent. "Our twenty-fifth amendment was put into place for situations such as these. The Vice President will submit in writing to Congress that the President is unable to perform his duties and will become the Acting President."

"And if President recovers?" the anchor asks.

"The Vice President stays Acting President until the President himself can submit in writing his ability to run the country."

"And do we know if this has taken place yet?"

"We do not. We're awaiting a press conference."

"Can you tell us what you think is happening behind the scenes?"

"Based on protocol, the Vice President, who was in route to the Summit, would have been diverted and taken to a secure location."

"How does the Vice President determine the President unable to serve?"

"I imagine he is being updated on the President's condition."

"Let's run that footage now," the anchor says, cutting him off. "We have Dr. Saul Penchant on the phone. Doctor, can you please watch this video and give us your professional opinion as to what condition you expect the President to be in?" He pauses and looks directly at the camera. "To our viewers, please note that this footage is of a graphic nature. Viewer discretion is advised."

I mute the sound, wanting to see what happened with my own eyes and not be swayed by someone else's opinion.

The President, surrounded by Secret Service, gets out of his limousine and turns to wave at the crowd gathered, who are being held back by construction barriers. Most are there to see the dignitaries as they arrive, but some are protesting the Summit. Just as the President turns back toward the entrance to the Summit, his body lurches. I pause the footage, rewind, and then watch it again in super-slow motion. The bullet appears to have entered the back of his neck. Most likely effective, but lower than I was taught to aim.

"They're saying he's been taken to the hospital," Lorenzo says into my ear, causing me to set down the remote. "What's your professional opinion?"

"A sniper, obviously, but based on where the President was hit, I'd say the shooter wasn't up very high. The trajectory of the bullet appears flatter than I would expect. For a kill shot, ideally you hit the brainstem, which controls all body functions. However, this shot didn't have optimal placement. If the President was lucky, the bullet may have passed clean through his neck."

"And if he was unlucky?"

"It hit a major artery or the spinal cord."

"How could someone do that? Security around the President is so tight."

"Same way they almost got you. There's no possible way the Secret Service can control every single window in the area. All it takes is one spot. One shot. Not that hard to do."

"Are you saying you could do it?"

"I could definitely do it. Quite frankly, shooting him wouldn't be that hard. Getting away with it is another story."

"So you think they will catch the assassin?"

"Depends on how good he is."

"Would they catch *you*?" he asks, a smile in his voice.

"The plan would be to *not* get caught."

"So you were trained to shoot like that?"

"I have very good skills with all types of weapons from varying distances, but I'm a much better shot at close range."

"Thank God for that," he says.

I hear Juan speaking to him again then Lorenzo says, "I'm afraid I have to go now, Huntley. I'm being called into an emergency meeting. Take care, my love."

AFTER WE END the call I sit at the bar, processing. I should be worried about our President and what it means for our country, but my thoughts are on Lorenzo. Two things he said took me by surprise, the first being that he still cares for me. The second being that Daniel somehow found out about me being on the yacht by myself and managed to convince the crew he was to join me.

"Would you care for a drink, Contessa?" Marco, one of the stewards asks, joining me in the salon.

"Got anything for a hangover?" I laugh. "How are you feeling today?"

"Remind me not to party with you," he says, relaxing his stiff posture. "You're an instigator."

"What's that supposed to mean?"

"It means you encouraged us to do shots, but did not partake in them yourself."

"I most certainly did, but I am not stupid enough to think I can match shots with someone of your body weight."

He looks down, patting his very firm stomach, and gives me a smile. Marco is funny, a great dancer, and likes to party. "Are you saying I'm fat?"

"I'm simply stating that you weigh more than I do."

His eyes move slowly down my body as his smile curls upward. "True."

"Can I ask you something in confidence, Marco?"

"Of course, Contessa."

"When did Daniel arrive on the Royal Yacht?"

"Just before you did. We were not notified in advance of his presence, but were ordered by the King to accommodate your every desire."

"And what made you think I desired Daniel?"

"He said he was to meet you aboard," he replies, as he moves behind the bar to make me a drink.

THE FACT THAT Daniel lied concerns me, and I wonder what that says about his character. Considering I've lied to him repeatedly, I shouldn't really judge, but I do. I have good reasons to lie. He doesn't.

With a concoction Marco calls "Hair of the Dog" in hand, I make my way down to the pool deck and spend a few minutes drinking it while watching Daniel carve through the water.

"Look at that," his trainer says as I approach. "The butterfly is the most physically demanding of all strokes and purely competitive, but when well executed is a thing of beauty. Daniel's perfect body movements are poetry in motion."

I can't argue with that, but I'm probably not focusing on the same thing he is. I'm focused on Daniel's perfectly formed shoulders and his sheer power.

"He holds the world record in the 200-meter butterfly," the trainer continues, "but I think he could break it at the Olympics this year." He looks directly at me. "*If* he's not distracted."

I ignore his comment, walk to the end of the pool, slip off my robe, and jump directly in Daniel's path.

Then I realize it was a stupid move because he's coming at me fast and doesn't appear to see me.

As I prepare to jump out of the way, he dives down, grabs me around the waist, kisses my stomach, then pops out of the water.

"My trainer is going to be pissed you interrupted my session," he says, pulling off his goggles and lowering his lips to my shoulder. "But I love it."

"Daniel, we need to talk. In private," I say, then I extricate myself from his hold and climb out of the pool.

As I step onto the pool deck, Marco is there, holding out a fresh robe for me to slip over my bikini.

Daniel gets out of the pool, wraps a towel loosely around his waist, and follows me to the owner's suite where I'm staying, ignoring shouts from his trainer to get his butt back into the pool.

"What's up?" he asks, sliding the towel off his hips and running it through his wet hair.

"How did you know I would be on the Royal Yacht?"

"Ellis told me when I went to your villa. Ari was having a party with only beautiful women on the guest list."

"So why didn't you stay there and party?"

"Because you were the only beautiful woman I was looking for. I needed to see for myself that you were okay, and I wanted to apologize for the bathroom."

"You never apologized."

He gives me a grin. "Well, I'm really not sorry for the bathroom. I wanted you. Now I have you."

"I just spoke to Lorenzo. He wasn't pleased to learn you were on his boat."

Daniel unties my robe and slides his hands inside, gripping my hips and bringing them toward his. Normally, I love his cockiness and find his take-charge ways appealing, but not now. I back away from him and readjust my robe over my bikini.

"You're mad?"

"I don't like to be lied to."

"I never lied to you."

"You told me you were my party."

"And I was," he says, flashing his dimples. "And it was one hell of a party. We spent the entire first twelve hours in my bed. If my trainer hadn't arrived, it would have been longer."

I knead my fingers into my eyebrows, calming myself down. It's clear that I am not well trained on one thing: relationships. No surprise. I'm supposed to avoid them. I'm only supposed to have meaningless sex—which is all the gorgeous man in front of me was ever supposed to be.

And how I need to keep it.

"I'll talk to Lorenzo," he finally says. "Is he mad at you? I assumed that you two were over since you weren't together after the kidnapping. Do you need to talk about it? Were you badly traumatized?"

"Isn't that something you should have asked me earlier? I didn't even hear from you after the kidnapping. You didn't even seem to care I was still alive."

"Of course I cared, but I'm the Vice President's son. I got shot with a tranquilizer dart and knocked out. I was either in the constant care of doctors or being asked a million questions."

"Like what?"

"Like what I remembered."

"And what was that?"

"Why are you asking me all these questions?"

"Because it happened to both of us. Wouldn't it be normal to talk about it? Were you at all worried about me? I was kidnapped, threatened at gunpoint. I saw people get shot. Yet, for four days, there was no word from you. Not even a single text."

"I'm sorry," he says, putting his head down. "I wasn't allowed."

"By who?"

"You came onto the scene quickly. There were some people in the government who were questioning you and Ari."

"So they took your phone?"

"They advised me not to have contact with you until they cleared your background."

"Maybe they should have done that before we had sex," I say, smarting. I'm mad. Worked up in the same way I was that night at The Casino when I was upset with both him and the Prince. Mad at people I'm not even supposed to have feelings for in the first place.

That's it.

My mission in Montrovia is over.

My relationships with both Lorenzo and Daniel should be as well.

He reaches out to touch my face, but I bob my head to the side so that he misses.

"I can't deal with drama right now, Huntley. I have to focus on my training."

"And I'm a distraction. I know. Your coach already told me so. Maybe you training here isn't a good idea."

"You are mad."

"It doesn't really matter, Daniel." I throw my hands up in the air, wondering why I'm even fighting with him when there is something more important I need to tell him. "That's really not even what I wanted to talk to you about." I grab the remote off the nightstand and flip on the TV. "The President of the United States was just shot."

"Jack was shot?" he asks, calling President John F. Hillford, Jr. by his nickname.

"Do you know him well?"

"Pretty well. What did Lorenzo say about it? Does he

know anything?"

"We were talking on the phone when he was informed of the news. He didn't have any details."

"Turn it up!" he yells out, as the picture flashes to the
White House Press Room, and his father steps behind
the podium.

I do as he asks and watch as he backs up and slowly
sits on my bed. I may be spending time with Daniel on
the boat, but I insisted on separate living quarters. I
couldn't bring myself to sleep with Daniel in Lorenzo's
suite.

His father speaks. "As most of you probably have
already heard, the President of the United States was shot
outside the entrance to the International Summit. We're
still awaiting details on his condition, but we know that
his life is in grave danger. I ask that you pray not only for
your President, but for his wife, Blair, and his daughters,
Cara and Isabelle. And for his parents, the former
President John Hillford, Senior and his wife, Betty.
Although he is the leader of our great nation, he is, first
and foremost, a husband, a father, and a son.

"It's too early in the investigation to know who is
behind the shooting, but rest assured, we will find those
responsible and bring them to justice. May God bless the
President, and may God bless the United States of
America," he says, concluding his speech.

"Mr. Vice President," a reporter says. "Are you the

Acting President?"

Daniel's father closes his eyes and nods. He's visibly upset. "Yes, while the President is incapacitated, I am Acting President."

"What about the shooter? Has there been an arrest?"

"I can't comment on the investigation, other than to say it is open, and I've received no definitive judgment on the shooter's motive or identity."

"Mr. Vice President, does that mean the shooter is still at large?"

"Yes, that is correct." The room breaks out in slight hysteria, reporters teetering on the edges of their chairs, eager to dissect this news on air. The Press Secretary steps in front of the podium as Daniel's dad moves away and says, "No further questions."

"I need to talk to my dad." Daniel runs into his stateroom to get his cell phone, comes back to sit next to me, and dials.

"Dad!" he says when his father answers. Because I'm sitting close, I can hear their conversation. "Are you safe?"

His father replies, "I'm in the White House. One of the safest places in the world."

"I just saw your press conference. How is Jack?"

"Not good, son."

"And do you really not know who the shooter was? Has no one taken credit?"

"The shooter was an assassin. And a very good one, since we can't find a single shred of evidence. Are you at your training facility?"

"No, I'm on Prince Lorenzo's yacht in Ibiza."

"You mean *King* Vallenta?"

"Yeah, whatever."

"I want you back in Washington," his father says as I hear a chopper off in the distance.

I go outside to investigate.

The chopper lands on the yacht's helipad, and Lorenzo gets out looking sexy as ever in an all black suit, black spread collared shirt, and shiny Italian loafers.

"What are you doing here?" I ask, greeting him with a tight hug. It's only been a few days since I've last seen him, but it feels like much longer.

"I'm told Daniel needs to get back to the States," he says, giving me cheek kisses.

"Are you sure you don't just want him off your boat?" I whisper.

He winks at me in reply.

When Daniel joins us on the helipad, Lorenzo cups his shoulder, like they are still buddies. "It seems your Secret Service would prefer to have you in America rather than out on my boat with all that's going on. My father and President Hillford were friends, so I will be departing for America shortly. Would you like a ride home on the Royal Montrovian Jet?"

"Yes, I would," Daniel replies gratefully. "Thank you."

THE FORMER DEAN of Blackwood Academy storms through the Black X headquarters and barges into the office of their leader, immediately shouting, "Did you conspire to kill the President?"

"What are you talking about, old man?" the leader asks.

"The President of the United States was just shot. It's all over the news."

"Well, that's quite the interesting plot twist," the leader replies, tilting his head thoughtfully.

"What do you mean?" The former Dean calms himself down, nervously smoothing the front of his trousers with his hands. "You didn't answer my question."

"No, I didn't."

"You said he was their pawn. You wanted him dead!"

"Just because I wanted him dead, doesn't mean *I* did it," the leader states. "The man has a lot of enemies in the world. Was it a terrorist attack?"

"No group has claimed responsibility as of yet. But it only happened in the last hour."

"What else do you know?" the leader interrogates. "Have you called your contact at the CIA?"

"I have a call into him, but I would expect he is a little busy at the moment."

"Why don't you go over there, visit an old friend for

lunch?"

"Because they all think I'm dead?" The former Dean can't help but give the leader the kind of eye roll that probably makes him look like his favorite former student.

"Send the Ghost to my office and cancel Huntley and Ari's vacation. I want them back on American soil." The leader then puts his nose down and starts tapping away on his keyboard. "I'm going to hack my way into Langley and see what I can find out."

WHEN WE GET to the palace, Ari is there waiting for us. I give him a hug. "I missed you. I take it you heard the news?" I ask, the two of us staying outside to chat.

"I missed—" He's interrupted as we simultaneously get a text from our personal concierge, meaning one of the Kates.

> **Concierge:** *We have secured your usual hotel suite in D.C. Please return to the States immediately.*

Ari smiles at me as he types into his phone.

> **Ari:** *We'll be staying at our father's estate. And we'll have guests, including the King of Montrovia and his entourage of 10.*
> **Concierge:** *I'm not sure that can be arranged on such short notice.*
> **Ari:** *I have a key and was told the house is always fully staffed.*
> **Concierge:** *I'll get back to you.*

Ari: No need. Just tell them to prepare for our arrival.

"Can we do that?" I ask him.

"Of course we can. I'll take care of this. Why don't you go inside and find out what time we're leaving."

As I MAKE my way down the hall to Lorenzo's study, I hear his voice. "What are your intentions regarding Huntley?"

I stop in my tracks, wondering who he's talking to.

Then I hear Daniel speak. "I have no intentions," he states, which hurts more than expected.

"Seriously?" Lorenzo asks.

"It's new and fun. A little early for intentions."

"Not as far as I'm concerned. As an honorable gentlemen and as your friend, you need to know that I will be doing my best to court her."

"Court her? More like bed her. Is that why you're all bent out of shape, because she hasn't slept with you?"

"She's different," Lorenzo states.

"Sure she is," Daniel agrees. "May the best man win."

We ARRIVE AT the airport with numerous personnel in tow, including Lorenzo's personal secretary, his communications secretary, his foreign affairs advisor, an operations manager, and six bodyguards. I wondered why we didn't use their private airstrip, but now I see why.

The plane we will be traveling on is an Airbus 380 that is quite large.

Instead of boarding via air stairs or a jetway, we walk underneath the plane, where a clear glass elevator is waiting to whisk us up inside the jet.

"I'm pretty sure I've seen everything now," Ari says.

"Or not," Daniel counters as the elevator doors side open and we get our first glimpse of the plane's interior—specifically the floating glass staircase that greets us.

"We're on a heightened state of security with what's going on in the world," Juan says firmly, leading us to a lush lounge area. "Please take your seats for an immediate departure."

AFTER WE'VE TAKEN off and reached cruising altitude, Lorenzo leans over and whispers, "May I give you a tour? I would have liked to give you one before the flight, but there wasn't time."

The King's advisors have moved into the dining room where they are following the news channels of the world, and Ari and Daniel are asleep in their seats.

"Your plane is quite luxe. I've seen pictures of Air Force One, and it seems very utilitarian compared to this."

"The President of the United States is a paid position. Important, but not quite the same as being part of a centuries long Royal Family." He takes my hand and leads me up the staircase. "This is the sleeping floor and consists of four staterooms, the largest of which is mine."

He opens the door, allowing me to enter the room first. It features a king-sized bed, private sitting area, mini bar, and a spa-like bathroom.

"This is beautiful," I gush.

He pushes me against the wall in the bathroom and kisses me hard, like he did in the tunnel.

I shouldn't be kissing him back.

I know I shouldn't be.

But I am.

Because I need to know that his kiss feels the same. That the passion I felt before the kidnapping is still there.

When Daniel cornered me in the bathroom at the Queen's Ball, I couldn't have sex with him. I told myself it was because of my mission but, really, it was because of my growing feelings for Lorenzo. If I'm being honest, I was a little disappointed to find Daniel on the yacht. I had held out hope that Lorenzo would be joining me, and it broke my heart a little because I thought it meant he had no further romantic interest in me. That we were over before we even got started.

"I can't do this," I say.

"Yes, you can. Your lips betray your true feelings."

"That's why I can't do this. I'm sorry."

"Don't be sorry, my darling. I was nervous to kiss you. Afraid the passion would be gone." We gaze into each other's eyes. He sighs. "I am prepared to be in an open relationship with you."

"An open relationship?"

"Yes, as you Americans say, no strings."

"Lorenzo, no."

"Huntley, I am open-minded when it comes to sex. I will see you when you allow me to, and I will cherish every moment we are together. And when we are apart, if you choose to be in the company of others, that is acceptable."

I should take his offer. No strings is the perfect arrangement for me.

Except . . .

"You might be fine with it, Enzo, but I'm not."

"I don't understand. Our kiss was exquisite. You say you care for me."

"And that's exactly why I am not fine with it." He cradles my cheeks in his palms as tears fill my eyes. "I can't have you, but I couldn't bear to share you. Can we please just be friends?"

He kisses me, deeper this time.

"Of course we can, my sweet."

WE RELAX ON his bed, me eventually falling asleep. It's about a nine-hour flight to D.C. Although we left Montrovia in the morning, due to the time change, we land in the Capitol midday.

Upon arrival at Ares Von Allister's mansion, we are

greeted by a butler named Charles, who comes with the house. Apparently, Ellis is still holding down the fort in Montrovia.

"Welcome to Le Chateau de Luminere, or House of Light," Charles says. "Built with French craftsmanship in 1927 on five acres of land and expanded over the years to around sixteen thousand square feet. In the renovation, your father combined the old world charm of the home with hi-tech conveniences and security. Would you like to enjoy a tour or would you prefer to be shown directly to your rooms?"

"I say we go to our rooms, freshen up, and meet down here for drinks. Then I'd love a tour."

"As would I," Lorenzo agrees.

"I'll just take a drink now," Daniel states. "The Secret Service is picking me up within the hour. I'm to report to One Naval Observatory immediately."

"Well, it won't take you long to get there, at least," the butler says. "The Vice President's home is only a hop, skip, and a jump from here. Five minutes or so by car."

WE DECIDE TO have drinks first, but soon Daniel and Lorenzo are splitting their focus between phone conversations and the television.

Ari leads me out to the courtyard to speak in private. "So much for a few weeks off," he says.

"When do you think we will get our mission?"

"Soon, I suspect."

"So, did you have fun at your party?" I ask, one eyebrow raised in amusement.

A wide grin breaks out across his face. "Yes. I'm sad our vacation was cut short."

"Do you really have a key to this house?"

"Yes, I do." He holds out a key. "And I have one for you, too."

"The house is beautiful. Before, you mentioned a research facility on site. Can I see it?"

"Of course, and I'd like to do some digging into Ares. We were told his death was sudden, but he had numerous properties around the world, which he only recently liquidated. Same with his company. It sold just months before his death. Although, it's good for us. Can you imagine if we had to run a multi-billion dollar business?"

"Ari, we didn't really inherit it. We're pretending."

"And I told you, that's not true. Legally, at least for now, his estate is ours. But that's not why I brought you out here. Something's been bugging me since the kidnapping. Why did you lie to the British agent about who we work for?"

"I didn't lie. I work for Black X. Who do you work for?"

"The CIA."

"Are you sure about that?"

"What do you mean?"

"I mean, are you sure?"

He ponders my question for a few moments. "No, actually, I'm not. I've never been to the CIA offices. I was sent to train with them, but then halfway through, I received a mission."

"Who gave it to you?"

"No one. It was in my locker. Later, I got a call that said I was to report to an attorney's office where I would learn about my cover and that I would soon have a partner, who would play the role of my long-lost sister. Tell me when you first heard about Black X and everything you know about them."

"Just after my sixteenth birthday, I got a visit from my uncle. Well, technically, he wasn't really my uncle, just a friend of my parents. After they died, I went to Blackwood at his suggestion. I hadn't seen him in, like, four years, so I was surprised when he showed up. Anyway, he gave me a safety deposit box key and told me that I was free to leave Blackwood, but that he hoped I would stay and finish my training and education.

After he left, the Dean called me to his office and asked if I planned to stay. I told him yes, and that's when he told me the truth about my school. He said that it was created by Black X, an agency so covert even the President didn't know of its existence. Black X believed that the CIA started training their agents too late in life, usually after college, so they started Blackwood to train young, elite spies—who could move in social circles of the rich and powerful. He told me that Black X only recruits those from the school with truly exceptional talent, and that they were already impressed with my scores and skills. My graduation ceremony is this week. I didn't think I'd be able to attend, but now I'm hoping I can. Since you know about my cover, maybe they will let you come with me."

"Let me?"

"No one but students and instructors are allowed to attend graduations, for obvious reasons."

"What about the students' families?"

"If the students have families, they are not allowed to attend. We weren't allowed to talk about our families or tell each other our real names."

"So what did you call each other?"

"We had letters. I was X."

"X is the name you've gone by for the last six years?"

"Yes."

He studies me more closely. "That almost sounds like a behavior-modification program. Were they brainwashing you?"

"No, just stripping us of our identity. That's the point, right—anonymity?"

"Yeah, I guess. You seem normal."

"I am normal." I slug him in the arm. "Well, as normal as someone can be with my skill set."

"Do you know anything else about Black X?"

"They are small and elite, but well-funded and powerful." I decide if I should tell him the rest. Ari seems to know so much more about Ares and this whole cover thing than I do, sometimes I feel at a disadvantage.

"Go on," he urges, placing his hand gently on my forearm. "What else did he say?"

"I'm not sure if I should tell you the rest. It's not in my file. You think my parents were killed in a car accident, right?"

He narrows his eyes at me. "They weren't?"

"For our cover purposes, they were. In real life, they weren't." My voice cracks. If he's going to be my partner, this is something he should know about. I'd hate to have it affect one of our missions. "My mother was a spy who was shot point-blank by an assassin."

"I'm sorry—"

"In front of me."

"Oh my God."

"A few days later, my dad's car exploded. I got out, he didn't. Anyway, the Dean told me that Black X would understand my need for revenge and would help me achieve it. Working for them immediately became my goal. My focus. To be good enough for them to want me. Because deep down I knew that the CIA would probably not allow me to go rogue and kill my mother's assassin."

"That's your goal?"

"Personally, yes."

"What about professionally?"

"I want to be the best."

"I'm sure it's painful to discuss, but did the assassin not see that you were there?"

"I was behind him. He had my mother down on her knees with the gun pointed at her head. I shot him in the shoulder just as he shot and killed her. Then we fought. I got away. I learned from Terrance while we were in Montrovia that my parents were both spies. Before that I thought they worked in international finance."

Ari sits down slowly—clearly shocked. "Why didn't you tell me?"

"The real question is why didn't anyone tell *me* they were spies. If Black X is so powerful, why did they keep it from me?"

"Maybe they didn't want to add to your grief. Maybe they were trying to protect you. You still haven't answered my question."

"I wasn't sure if I could trust you."

"What changed your mind?"

"When I told Intrepid I worked for Black X, you told me not to lie to him. I knew then that honesty is important to you. When I asked how you were notified of your mission, you told me yours had unicorns and rainbows or something. Mine came in an envelope with a monogrammed X wax seal. I asked the Dean if it was from whom I thought it was. He told me yes."

"So you really don't know much about them, either?"

"No."

"That worries me."

"Why?"

"What if we're playing for the wrong team?"

"I don't know how that could be," I disagree. "We saved the Prince of Montrovia. That was a good thing."

"True. It will be interesting to see what they have for us next." He glances behind me. I turn around and see Daniel coming outside.

"I have to go. The Secret Service is here."

"I'll walk you out," I say, escorting him back through the house.

Two black SUVS are idling in the circular driveway, one with its door open. Two men in dark suits, dark shades, and earpieces are flanking it.

Daniel pulls me close and whispers in my ear. "Leave your balcony door open tonight. I'll ditch them if I can."

"If you can ditch them, they aren't doing their job," I whisper back.

"We'll see," he says with a cocky grin. "Or you could come crash my party."

"You're having a party?"

"A very private one."

I give him a playful smack and roll my eyes at him. "With your trainer?"

This time he sighs. "You know I meant just you and me. But you're right. I do have to meet my trainer very early in the morning."

One of the men clears his throat, anxious to get Daniel home.

Daniel smacks my butt and says, "See ya."

A short time later, I get a text.

> **Daniel:** *You are cordially invited to dinner at the Vice President's house.*
>
> **Me:** *Isn't your dad kind of busy, like running our country in its time of crisis?*
>
> **Daniel:** *Yes, but Mom said he needed to come home for dinner.*
>
> **Me:** *I don't think I can. Lorenzo is here.*
>
> **Daniel:** *You're going to turn down the chance to meet the Acting President of the United States?*
>
> **Daniel:** *I want you to meet my parents. Please.*
>
> **Me:** *Let me see if I can figure something out.*
>
> **Daniel:** *I'm sure Ari can entertain your guest. Why don't you join them after dinner? I'm sequestered here until further notice.*
>
> **Me:** *Maybe. Dress code?*
>
> **Daniel:** *Naked.*
>
> **Me:** *Can't wait to take photos of the Spear family's naked dinner party and post it to my social media.*
>
> **Daniel:** *Fine. Something deliciously sexy.*
>
> **Me:** *What will your mother be wearing?*
>
> **Daniel:** *Either scrubs or a formal gown. One can never tell.*

The Second Lady is a highly sought after neurosurgeon and one of the few in history to keep her day job while her husband is in office.

> **Me:** *You are no help whatsoever.*
> **Daniel:** *It's just our family, so casual.*
> **Me:** *Thank you.*
> **Daniel:** *So . . . Enzo didn't seem mad at me.*
> **Me:** *He wasn't exactly happy.*
> **Daniel:** *What's the deal with you two, anyway?*
> **Me:** *Pretty much the same as it is with you. New and fun.*
> **Daniel:** *You overheard our conversation?*
> **Me:** *I did.*

LORENZO AND HIS staff have taken over the formal dining room. Ari and I are headed out the front door when he steps out and says, "Where are you going?"

"Our father had a research facility on the property. I've never seen it."

"I'm nearly finished with my call, may I join you?"

I look at Ari, his initial tick quickly replaced with a smile. "We'll wait for you out front," he says.

"You didn't want him to come?" I ask once we're outside.

"I suppose since he knows the truth about us, it's okay. Do you trust him?"

"Explicitly."

"We're in espionage, Huntley. We're not supposed to trust anyone."

"What about each other?"

He narrows his eyes at me. "Do you have any more secrets you need to tell me about?"

"I can't think of any. What about you?"

"Nothing important."

The massive front doors open, and Lorenzo strides out alone.

"No guards?"

"Are you going to try to kill me?" he asks, taking my hand and kissing it.

"Depends how nice you are to me," I reply with a laugh.

We follow a stone path through a beautiful English garden, which includes a lake and sweeps of gently rolling lawn. Beyond the landscaping are groves of trees, giving the illusion that we are in the countryside as opposed to the middle of a major metropolitan city. We traverse over a stone bridge and through a heavily treed area, then a building comes into view.

"Before Ares became a recluse, numerous employees worked in this facility." He points to an empty guard shack. "They entered from the street, there."

When we get to the front of the building, something clicks in my memory.

"I think I've been here before," I mutter.

"When?" Lorenzo simply asks.

"It's pretty nondescript," Ari counters. "It probably just reminds you of somewhere."

"Yeah, probably," I agree, even though there's something nibbling on the corner of my thoughts. "I can't remember certain pieces of my past."

"Psychological trauma can cause gaps in memory," Lorenzo says. "With what you went through, that wouldn't be unusual."

"I don't know if I have gaps in my memory from that or if it's because I purposely haven't tried to remember."

"You try not to remember your parents?" Lorenzo asks.

"I remember seeing them die. That's enough."

"But you need to replace those memories with good ones."

"The good memories are too painful. I was counseled not to do that."

"You were told not to think about your parents?" Ari asks.

"We all were. It was part of our training. Focusing on being self-sufficient," I state.

Lorenzo and Ari both study me. It makes me uncomfortable, so I let go of Lorenzo's hand and make my way to the front door, hoping they will follow. I don't need to stand here and discuss my psychological well-being.

I'm a covert agent and an assassin. There's obviously something about me that will never be normal.

Thankfully, they don't press the subject.

Ari punches some numbers into a keypad, and the front door opens.

"This facility seems very secure. Keypads, cameras," Lorenzo states.

"Ares specialized in military research and holds numerous patents on those products, which were then produced by his company and sold to governments around the world."

"Like what kinds of things?"

Ari waves his hand around the entry, which is full of framed photos of mechanical design drawings next to their finished product.

"Intelligence, surveillance, and reconnaissance drones were his greatest achievement, which are now weaponized with the ability to carry multiple payloads, pull high G-forces, and hit high risk targets without jeopardizing pilots."

"He was a war monger," I mutter.

"He didn't design weapons," Ari counters, "and his drones have saved thousands of lives. His company also supplied the government with an information and communication lifeline. Secure communications, radar jamming, and disablement were just some of the things he worked on. Then there are the training and simulation games. Remote control bomb disposal robots. He also dabbled in espionage." He walks down a hall and points to another section of wall. "Although they look big in the drawings, what you see here are tiny bugs and tracking devices."

I think about how Terrance said our villa was wired.

It'd be sort of fitting if they used my fake father's stuff to do so.

We stroll through what was a once bustling facility, my mind clearly picturing it—the labs full of men in white coats huddled around stainless steel tables, classical music playing, and a dog. *What was the dog's name?* I'm sitting on the floor, her chin across my lap, petting her long soft fur and telling her my name is Calliope and that people call me Callie sometimes, just like they do her.

"Caliper," I mutter.

"Yes, a carbon ceramic disc for automotive applications was one of his earliest patents," Ari replies.

"It was? Are you sure?" My eyes get huge.

I cover my face, not noticing the tears sliding down my cheeks, as I picture my parents standing in the hall. My dad dressed in a navy suit, joking about the dog shedding all over it but petting her anyway. My mom is wearing what I called her mom uniform, a striped blazer, collared shirt, and jeans. Her hair is up and recently dyed a dark chestnut color. The dog licks her face, and she laughs—

"Huntley, what's wrong?" Lorenzo grabs my arms. "Why are you crying?"

I shake my head, pushing the memory away.

"I've been here before. With my parents. There was a dog named Caliper. A beautiful Golden Retriever who everyone in the office said was an attention whore. She laid her head in my lap and let me pet her."

"When was this?" he asks, gently taking my hand.

I shake my head. "I don't remember."

"That's surprising," Ari says. "Do you remember anything else? Did you meet Ares Von Allister when you were here?"

I shake my head. "I don't think so."

Ari leads me into an office whose walls are covered with more photos. "This is Ares. Does he look familiar?"

"Familiar, yes. There was a photo of him in my dossier, but I don't feel like I've ever met him personally. He certainly knew a lot of important people, though," I state as I go down the line. "Presidents, heads of state, entertainers, athletes. Look, Enzo, here's a photo of him with your dad. I remember he said they knew each other."

Lorenzo tightens his grip on my hand. Seeing his father looking so young and healthy understandably affecting him.

"I'm sorry," I whisper.

"Alright, enough of memory lane," Ari says after searching numerous drawers only to find them empty. "I thought there would be more here."

"I'm sure once he sold the company, everything was cleaned out," Lorenzo says.

"You're probably right. I have one more place I want to see. There's a detached garage on the property that I'm told still houses his car collection. We may need something to drive while we are here."

Lorenzo's face lights up, and so does mine, but for different reasons. He wants to see the cars. I want to get out of this building.

There's something I don't like about it. Maybe it's just that it's sad. That the lifetime achievements of a brilliant man are reduced to this upon his death. All the money, fame, and power he had didn't matter. He ended up dying alone.

I think that's my biggest fear. A bullet. A knife. A bomb. Poof, I'm gone. And no one cares.

Which is exactly what I'm supposed to want. What I was trained to want. If there is no one at home who cares, I'm willing to take risks others wouldn't.

Ari locks up then we follow the path back toward the house. Behind the home and off to the north is a beautiful redwood and steel garage.

Ari enters another code and the doors open, revealing what looks more like a car museum. Highly polished wood floors with not a speck of dust or tread mark. Steel beams supporting an open vault ceiling.

Rows of exotic cars, all parked at an angle, greet us.

"Holy moly. My second favorite F-word!" Ari exclaims, looking like a kid in a candy store.

Lorenzo shares his excitement. "I can't believe all these Ferraris are just sitting here."

I stand in the center of the room. There are two rows of cars on each side of me, eleven cars in each row for a total of forty-four, and from what I can tell, every single one of them a Ferrari.

"Did he not like any other brand?" I wonder.

"A collection like this would be of more value because it's limited to one manufacturer," Lorenzo states.

At the side of each car is a placard noting the year and model of the car, how many of each were made, and the year Ares purchased it. The cars appear to be in order by year of purchase rather than make, the first one noted as *Ares' daily driver*. It's a black 1990 Testarossa. Next to it sits his second purchase, a 1993 Ferrari F40 Berlinetta with distinctive 'triple black' paintwork. And so on.

"Look at this one!" Lorenzo yells out. "It's a 1962 Ferrari 250 GTO. I think this car alone is worth close to forty million."

I follow the line down to Ares' last purchase—a gorgeous 2016 red F60 America. I pop the door open, slide in, and start it. The engine springs to life with the kind of smooth, throaty sound that brings big boys to their knees. Ari and Lorenzo rush over.

"It only has twenty miles on it. I bet he never got to drive it."

"We should fix that," Ari says. "What do you say, Lorenzo? Shall we take her for a spin?"

"You two have fun." I glance at my watch. "I have to get dressed for dinner. Leave it in the driveway for me. I'll take it to the Vice President's home."

"Are you ditching us?" Ari asks, although with the

smile plastered on his face, I highly doubt he cares.

"Yes, Daniel invited me. It's not too often you get a chance to meet the Vice President." Lorenzo rolls his eyes, which causes me to laugh. "Okay, maybe not for you. Anyway, I'll meet you back here for a night cap."

Lorenzo steps away from the car and takes me into his arms. "You're coming home without Daniel?"

"Yes."

A smile lights up his face. "That makes me very happy."

"SHE REMEMBERED THE dog's name," the Ghost says, replaying the recent video footage from Ares Von Allister's former lab. "Do you think she will remember the rest? Could her memory be returning?"

"We can only hope," the leader of Black X replies. "She could very well be the key to unlocking their ultimate plan. The psychiatrist said she had a form of dissociative amnesia that caused her to block out the time period around the traumatic event. Her case was unusual because this amnesia typically leaves the patient unable to remember any personal information. She did not have such losses and retained those memories. The man believed she was simply stubborn."

"And you wouldn't allow him to medicate her."

"It would have done nothing but impede her training."

"If we could discover where they were before her

mother's death, it could greatly help our cause."

The man nods. "That it would, but she must re-member on her own."

WHEN I ARRIVE back at the house, I find not only my luggage from Montrovia unpacked and all my clothing hung, but I find new items in the closet, as well. Gotta love the Kates.

I had no idea what to wear tonight, but on each new item is a tag stating what kind of event it would be appropriate for and what to pair with it. There is everything from new bikinis to new ball gowns.

I work my way through the rack, finding a simple navy cotton shirtdress with a cute fit-and-flare profile. The tag suggests it would be perfect for a casual lunch or dinner and to pair it with the navy 'Kiki' fringe Jimmy Choo sandal and a red, white, and blue embroidered Gucci shoulder bag. Once I locate the proper shoes, I put everything on, spin around, and look in the mirror. Gone is the girl from Blackwood Academy who always had her hair in a bun to keep it from getting in the way of her training and who dressed in an all black uniform for years. And although I will admit that the upkeep of looking this way takes a lot of time, I kind of like this girl. She looks like she's having fun.

And I am. I'm in my element.

Successfully completing my first mission will hopefully lead to more excitement, danger, and intrigue.

And pretending to be Huntley Von Allister is turning out to be a much better gig than sleeping in sketchy safe houses and traveling by public transportation.

It's like the best of both worlds. The tricky part will be completing my missions without blowing my cover.

At seven, I step out the front door to find the Ferrari I asked for in the drive. Lorenzo and Ari are nowhere to be seen, but I can hear the sound of a throaty motor in the distance. Knowing them, they are probably going to take *all* the cars out for a spin.

LOCATED ON THE northeast grounds of the U.S. Naval Observatory, the Vice President's home is a beautiful, nineteenth-century Queen Anne-style house. Upon arrival, I'm greeted by Daniel and his mother, Dr. Amanda Spear, in a large traditional entry with yellow and white striped wallpaper, thick crown molding, wood floors, and oriental carpets. The house has a nautical, casual air.

Daniel's mother is indeed dressed in scrubs, having just arrived home from the hospital. Daniel introduces us, then she excuses herself to go change.

"My father should be arriving shortly," Daniel says, looking tired. "I've been in meetings regarding my safety since I left your house. If the Secret Service had its way, I would not be participating in the Olympics this year, but that's not going to happen. Would you like to see my new training facility?"

"Sure."

He grabs a couple water bottles out of the kitchen fridge and tosses one in my direction. Then he leads me out the back door, under an arched pergola, and to the pool. "It's not as long as it should be, but it is what it is for now."

"You seem upset."

"I'm only a few weeks away from the Olympic try-outs and this is where I have to swim. It's not an Olympic-sized pool."

"Neither was the one on the Royal Yacht, but you managed."

"That was different," he says, flashing me a dimple and slipping his arms around my waist. "I was there with you. By the way, you look cute tonight."

"That's good. I was going for cute."

He laughs. "Usually, you look drop-dead sexy, but this dress has a school girl quality to it. For one, it's navy, which is the color of the uniforms from the parochial schools of my youth. For two, I think you're trying to impress my parents because you like me."

"I've been sleeping with you, Daniel. Of course I like you."

"I think it's more than that."

"Maybe I'm trying to look sweet, like the kind of girl

who *isn't* sleeping with their son. Although, they have to know how you get around."

"Not everything you read in the tabloids is true." I raise an eyebrow in his direction. "Fine, in my case, most of it is true. I'm a world-class athlete and I get a lot of women. It's one of the perks I enjoy. Is there anything wrong with that?"

"You're young and single. Of course there's nothing wrong with that. I know I'm certainly not ready to settle down."

"The Montrovian press seems to think otherwise."

"Yeah, well, they haven't photographed me with Lorenzo since the Ball, so I'm sure that will die down."

"And I posted a photo of us together on my social media," he says with a smirk.

"Daniel, my feelings are not a game to be won. And if you're doing that just to get back at the King, you're an even shittier friend than I thought."

He hangs his head. "I didn't do it for that reason. I just wanted . . ."

"Wanted what?"

"You to like me more. You turned me down in the bathroom, and what you said stung."

"Maybe I should just go."

"I don't bring many girls home, Huntley. I didn't ask you here to get you away from Lorenzo, I did it because I want them to meet you."

"I don't want to be in a relationship, Daniel. I just found out I have a brother. I can do all the things I used to dream about as a kid. I need to do those things, just like you need to go to the Olympics. Focus on your training. Your future. You get one shot at it. I don't want to be a distraction. But I'd love to be in the stands cheering you on when you win."

"You'll come to the Olympics?" he asks, his eyes brightening to their brilliant blue color.

"Absolutely."

The sound of a helicopter interrupts his leaning in to kiss me. "Sounds like Dad's home from work."

"Where does Marine Two land? Can we watch?"

He raises his eyebrows at me like I'm crazy.

"Although it may be an everyday occurrence to you, to most of us, it'd be a pretty cool thing to see."

He gives me a quick kiss, then grabs my hand.

"We'll have to hurry." We run up the back stairs and down a long hallway to a bedroom, where we rush to the window and pull open the curtains. "They will land on the lawn right across from here."

I watch in awe as the helicopter lands, and the Vice President gets out and walks, flanked by Secret Service, to his home.

"Come on, let's go downstairs."

"NICE CAR," ARE the first words spoken to me by the

Acting President of the United States.

"Thanks, it was one of my father's," I reply, shaking his hand. "I'm Huntley Von Allister."

"That was his first big break, you know," Daniel's father, Vice President Ryan Spear, says.

"What was?"

"Ares Von Allister is best known for his military inventions, but his first big financial deal was selling a high performance braking mechanism to Ferrari." He points at the wheel. "Take a closer look at the red caliper there."

I kneel down to inspect it, noticing for the first time the Von Allister company logo, a V and A layered over each other in a circular monogram that was prevalent at his facility. "That's pretty cool."

"I heard he had quite the Ferrari collection."

I nod. "I just saw it for the first time today. It is impressive."

We make our way into the house as Daniel's mother is coming down the staircase dressed in a soft teal wrap dress and sensible heels.

"You're late," she says to her husband and gives him a playful kiss. In one simple exchange, it's obvious how deeply they care for each other. "Grab a drink and join us in the dining room."

"My parents are on their way. They'll be staying with us for a few days," he says to his wife.

"Did you let the staff know?" she asks.

"Julie did," he says. "She said she texted you, as well."

She waves her hand. "Sorry, I forgot to look at my phone. I stopped by to see the First Lady before I left the hospital."

"How is she doing?"

"She's hanging in there, but his prognosis is not good. There's very little brain function. I feel so badly for her. I can't even imagine going through that. She feels so helpless. It's sad. There is literally nothing they can do but wait for him to pass."

"You don't think there's any chance of him recovering?"

"I'd say his odds are less than one percent and diminishing."

Daniel's father lowers his head and makes his way to the bar just as the front door bursts open due to a gust of wind catching the Secret Service agent who opened it off guard.

He grabs the door and announces, "Your parents have arrived."

A few moments later, the family is hugging each other in the entryway, and I'm introduced to Daniel's grandparents, Joseph Spear and his wife, Judith. After some small talk, we're seated in the dining room as dinner is ready to be served.

I'm next to Daniel on one side of the table, opposite his grandparents, and his mother and father are sitting at the heads of the table. I'm making polite conversation but am mostly just enthralled watching them interact. They seem very close, and I come to learn that while Daniel shares his mother's temperament, he owes his form and bright blue eyes to his father and grandfather. I know I'd sure as hell vote for either of the elder Spears. It's fun to see all three generations lined up, matching eyes, similar height and build, but with varying shades of hair color. Daniel's is dark, making the contrast of his eyes more distinct. His father's is a salt and pepper mix, and his grandfather's completely grey. Each stage of life equally attractive in different ways. While his grandfather seems more refined, his father seems to love the challenge of the game—another trait passed on to his son.

His mother exudes a strong confidence. She's smart, straightforward, and affable. I could see the political arena feeling like bullshit to her. I also suspect trust is extremely important to her. She's nice to me but slightly aloof. Or maybe that's just a natural reaction to all the girls who come and go from Daniel's life. She knows I won't last, so why bother getting to know me.

Grandma, on the other hand, loves me. Apparently, she follows the tabloids and knows of my relationship with Lorenzo, probably more reason why Daniel's mother doesn't care for me, and keeps me engaged in conversation.

A few moments after our soup dishes are removed and our main course placed in front of us, a phone vibrates.

"It's the First Lady," Dr. Spear says. "I need to take this." She steps into the hallway, speaks in hushed tones, then comes back in the room looking solemn. "The President passed away a few minutes ago. I gave her our sincere condolences."

She no more than gets the words out of her mouth when the Vice President's phone starts ringing. He answers, says he understands, and hangs up.

"I will be sworn in as President," he says numbly. "Shouldn't I get a few moments to mourn?"

"Are you required to have an official swearing in and an inaugural party?" Daniel asks. "All that pomp and circumstance would seem disrespectful considering the circumstances."

"No, that's only for elected Presidents. We have to put our grief aside for a few moments. Our country can't be without a leader." He smiles at his dad. "And how lucky I am to have my father, a judge, here to be able to do it for me."

Grandpa nods, his eyes filled with pride. "It would be my honor."

Very quickly the dining room is filled with the Vice President's staff. "Sir—"

"We've already been informed on the President's passing," Daniel's dad says. "Amanda just spoke to the First Lady."

"We need to get you sworn in immediately, sir."

"We'll need a Bible," Grandpa says.

"Let's all go into the study," Daniel's mother suggests.

Once in the study, Daniel's father scans a bookshelf. "I have multiple Bibles, but this one seems most appropriate."

Grandma gets tears in her eyes when he shows it to her. "That was the Bible my father gave to you when you became Governor. It's been in our family for generations."

We gather around and watch as the Honorable Joseph Spear places the Bible in his palm and holds it in front of his son. Acting Vice President Ryan Spear raises his right hand and places his left hand on the Bible.

"Repeat after me," the judge says. "I do solemnly swear that I will faithfully execute the Office of President of the United States, and will to the best of my ability, preserve, protect and defend the Constitution of the United States, so help me God."

After repeating the words, he shakes his head. "I have always dreamed of becoming President, but not in this way. Let's have a moment of silence for Jack."

THE NEW PRESIDENT of the United States is given hugs by his family, and I'm feeling both proud to be an American and lucky to have been able to witness this piece of history for myself.

"You'll need to address the nation," his advisor states.

"After that, I'll share a photo of the swearing in with the media."

"You arrange for a press conference, while we finish our meal," he replies. "I have a feeling it's going to be a long night."

AFTER DESSERT, I bid the family goodnight.

"I'm sorry our dinner was interrupted," President Spear says. "It was very nice to meet you."

"It was a pleasure to meet your family, as well. My condolences for your loss—and, I guess, congratulations."

The President nods his head solemnly, and Daniel walks me to my car.

"I can't believe that just happened," he says, pulling me into his arms. "It's almost surreal."

"I know. You are now the First Son."

"Which means even more Secret Service to deal with."

"But I bet the White House has a bigger pool."

He grins. "You're right. They do. It was built by Gerald Ford, who swam laps most every day."

"See, there you go."

"Do you have to leave?"

"We have house guests, remember?"

"Oh, trust me, I haven't forgotten that Lorenzo is sleeping across the hall from you. Just make sure it stays that way," he says, lowering his mouth to mine in a possessive kiss.

"I really have to go," I tell him, pulling my lips away and sliding in the car.

WHEN I ARRIVE back at the mansion, the butler informs me that Ari is out for the evening and that Lorenzo is in the theater room.

I slip my heels off and head that way, only to find Juan and Lorenzo both sound asleep, an action movie playing loudly in the background. I don't blame them.

They had been awake for almost twenty-four hours.

I quietly slip out of the room and am soon in my own bed.

MISSION: DAY TWO

EVEN THOUGH I was exhausted and fell asleep the second my head hit the pillow, my internal clock is messed up and I find myself wide awake at four in the morning.

I patter down the stairs, make a cup of coffee, and on my way back hear the sounds of a television coming from Lorenzo's room across the hall.

I go back downstairs, make another cup of coffee, return to the hall, and then gently knock on his door.

He answers wearing just a pair of pajama bottoms. Although his physique isn't as bulky as Daniel's, it's equally impressive.

I bite my lip. "Heard the television, thought you might want some coffee."

"Thank you. Would you like to come in?"

I walk into his room, set a cup of coffee on his nightstand, and climb onto his bed.

"Last night you were on the sidelines of history."

"Yeah, that was kind of crazy. We were sitting there eating dinner when they got the call. And within minutes we were in the study watching him being sworn in."

He turns his computer, showing me a photo of the swearing in. I'm standing next to Daniel looking very patriotic in my outfit choice.

"That photo of President Spear being sworn in will be in every history book printed from this day forward. With you in it."

"I wonder what the history books will say when they find out that Huntley Von Allister was not who she said she was, but rather a covert agent and trained assassin."

"And you have the Montrovian rumor mills buzzing again, Contessa." He flips to a Montrovian tabloid that's contemplating my relationship with Lorenzo. "They don't know what to think of you. First, you are photographed at the gala in Washington with Daniel, then spend a week being photographed with me."

"Are they calling me the orphan slut now?"

He laughs. "On the contrary, they are calling you a very lucky girl."

"I suppose. Two incredibly handsome men, vying for my heart. Which would be great if that were true."

"You don't think Daniel and I are vying for your

heart?"

"I think Daniel's only concern is for my body."

"He does not fancy you other than in his bed?"

I shrug. "He's very hot and cold. One minute he wants me to meet his parents and support him at the Olympics, the next he's telling me he likes no strings relationships because he can't be distracted during his training."

"That is the problem with American men. They are afraid to clearly state their intentions."

"Does the Playboy Prince usually state his intentions to the women he beds?" I roll my eyes.

"Actually, I do," he says, his heated gaze trailing down my body, which I realize now is very scantily clad in only a skimpy silk robe. "Would you like me to state my intentions toward you more clearly than I already have?"

"Um . . ."

He leans closer to me and says in his dreamy accent, "I desire you, Huntley, and am fully committed in my pursuit."

I grab the computer off his lap and click back to the article about President Spear's swearing in. Anything to change the subject. "I look sad in the picture."

"You do, as is appropriate in that situation."

"It was hard. You could feel his family's pride. Imagine your dad being sworn in as President." I glance at him and laugh. "Okay, so you probably don't have to imagine something like that. Anyway, there was the pride, but also the sorrow of losing their family friend. I suppose that's how you felt during your coronation. A lot of mixed emotions."

"That's exactly how I felt."

"So what did you do last night? What are your plans for today?"

"Ari and I had dinner. He went out after, and Juan and I watched a movie. Well, part of it. I fell asleep. I have a staff meeting this morning then a visit to the Embassy. There is a formal event at the Embassy this week. Would you be willing to accompany me?"

"I'd love to." I set my coffee on his nightstand. "I'm sleepy, but I can't sleep."

He holds his arm out, so I can snuggle up to him. The gesture causes my heart to do a little flip.

I should leave.

All my instincts and training are yelling at me to leave.

But I don't want to.

So I lie down next to him and enjoy the feel of his arms wrapped around me and his lips pressed against my temple. When I turn to face him, he kisses me. It's a slow, tentative kiss. Like he's dipping his toes in a pool to determine its temperature. When I run my hand through the back of his hair, he must decide it's warm and dives in, his tongue tangling with mine.

Our kissing quickly becomes heated, his hand sliding under my robe.

"Um?"

He stops kissing me, but his hand continues to caress my bare skin.

"Is my show of affection making you uncomfortable?"

"No, I just—"

"Do you wish I halt my advances?"

"Yes . . . no . . . maybe."

"Which is it, my sweet?"

My body, which had tensed, relaxes when he calls me that. I want to just sigh with happiness. What would I do if I weren't a spy? Probably allow myself to fall head over heels in love with him only to get heartbroken. Regardless of how dreamy he is, his reputation is for loving and leaving them.

Which makes me wonder why I don't just love him?

Not like fall for him, I mean experience him, sexually.

His hand glides down my arm. "You are not so uptight. You like words of love?"

But I can't do that, either. It was only a few days ago when I was last with Daniel. Even though sex is supposed to be only about pleasure, it doesn't feel right. I start to rise. "I think I better go back to my room."

"Don't go, Huntley," he says, holding his hands up in defeat. "I enjoy the pleasure of your company. Do you not wish to have a physical relationship with me?"

"I have a purely physical relationship with Daniel. It suits my lifestyle."

"And you aren't interested in a purely physical relationship with me?"

"I could never have a purely physical relationship with you, Lorenzo. The only reason I slept with Daniel on the yacht is because I thought we were over."

"So are we to start anew? Am I—as you Americans say it—back on first base with you?"

I laugh but feel like crying. I reach out and touch his handsome face then shake my head. "I can't have a physical relationship with you, because it would be my undoing."

"You already have me completely undone. I long to experience more with you. Every kiss is precious and exquisite," he says, his thumb tracing the line of my collarbone then moving to caress my face. When his knuckles graze my lips, I squeeze his hand and press my lips against it, enjoying the tenderness of the moment.

Then I jump off the bed, tears in my eyes. "I'm sorry. I have to go."

I run to my room, flop across my bed, and allow myself to dream of a different life.

Then I shake my head to clear my silly thoughts and

get in the shower.

I'M JUST GETTING dressed for the day when I get a text from Terrance. Just a single dot. Like maybe it was a butt-text. But then I run into the closet, grab my handbag, and pull out the phone he gave me.

I have seven missed calls from him over the last few days. I hadn't bothered to check it while I was on vacation.

I quickly choose his number—the only number—from the speed dial list.

"Sorry I missed your calls."

"We need to talk," he says. "About the thing you gave me. There's a bar in the Hay-Adams hotel called Off the Record. I'll be at a table by the fireplace. I was going to tell you to dress in a suit and blend in, but after last night, that's not possible. You might as well wear something outrageously sexy. Sit next to me on the couch, your back against the wall. Bring a big enough purse that I can put something into it. Then we'll have lunch and flirt."

"Okay. What time?"

"I'm already here."

A QUICK GOOGLE search tells me the hotel is directly across from the White House and often filled with congressional leaders. Upon arrival, I'm directed downstairs. Terrance was right, most everyone I've seen so far is wearing a suit.

I chose a grey spaghetti strap dress with a swingy skirt in a slinky jersey fabric. The front of the dress is a crossover style, and there is a small triangular cutout at the waist that adds to the sex appeal. On the hanger was a little card that suggested for daytime I pair it with the Valentino Rockstud butterfly-embroidered tie-dye tote and the multi-color trim, wedge-heel Louboutins.

So I did.

When I pulled the pieces out of the closet, I didn't think it all matched, but I have to admit, it looks good together. And I may be slightly obsessed with how cute this tote is.

I spot Terrance in his seat by the fireplace and quickly scan the room for potential threats and possible exits. Then I stop myself. I can assume that Terrance wouldn't be here if he didn't feel it were safe, and I shouldn't look calculating as I walk through the room. I am Huntley Von Allister, new billionaire heiress, who has not a care in the world other than how to spend her money. I'm making my way through the lunch crowd when I hear my name and turn to see Senator Bill Callan waving at me from the bar.

I walk over to greet him.

"Huntley, my dear, how are you?"

"I'm well. Did you and Sissy have a pleasant time in

the Caymans?"

"It was enjoyable, but I'm afraid we cut our trip short and came home when the President was shot."

"It's just horrible," I say. "I can't believe this happened in our great country."

"Me either. I was actually going to try to reach you today. Are you and Aristotle staying at your late father's home here in D.C.?"

"Yes, we are."

"I'd like to invite you to a dinner party my wife and I are having in Georgetown tonight. Are you and your brother free?"

I try to think of a way out of it. I can only imagine how boring one of his weeknight parties would be. Although, he's a senator, and the more contacts we make, the better for our cover, right? "Yes, I believe we are."

"Perfect. I will have Sissy messenger the invitation to your home." He turns to the man seated next to him, who I instantly recognize from my studies. "Where are my manners? Huntley, I'd like to introduce you to the Director of the CIA, Mike Burnes."

I put on a big smile and try not to look nervous. "Wow. I guess the write-ups about this bar were correct. It's nice to meet you, Mr. Burnes."

"Mike will be at the dinner party this evening. I sincerely hope you can join us. You and your brother were delightful dinner companions."

"Thank you. We'll see you then. Now, if you'll excuse me, I'm supposed to be meeting someone."

They say goodbye, and I work my way through to the back of the room where Terrance is waiting.

When he stands to greet me, I kiss his cheek and whisper, "Did you see who I just spoke to?"

"I did. If anyone asks, we met at the Montrovian Royal Casino," he whispers back.

"It's so good to see you again," I say, knowing that we have to be careful.

"So, Huntley, remember that vintage bag you wanted me to track down for you when I told you I was an internet whiz?"

"Um, yes." I go along with his ruse, knowing he's talking about the locket not some stupid bag. "Did you have any luck?"

"I did."

A waiter interrupts him and asks for our drink order. I pause for a second. I'm not of legal drinking age, but Huntley Von Allister would order something.

"What do you think I'd like?" I ask the waiter flirtatiously.

He doesn't miss a beat. "I'd go with the pear martini."

I smile and give a little clap. "Oh, that sounds yummy."

"Would you like a sugared rim?"

"Of course," I reply, even though I know the drink is just a prop and I won't take more than a few sips.

"And for you, sir?" he asks Terrance.

Terrance raises an eyebrow in my direction. "You buying?"

"Sure. Why not?"

"Then I'll have the JW Blue Label," he says. "And we'll share the macaroni and cheese fritters and the salted caramel creme brûlée to start." While he's ordering, he discreetly slides an envelope into my handbag then switches to sit across from me. "So I can stare into those gorgeous eyes of yours," he says, before the waiter leaves. Terrance looks quite dapper here, dressed in a navy suit, white spread collar, and a traditional red tie.

"Rumor has it the man can read lips," Terrance says. "So I'll talk and you say random things in reply to make it look like we're having fun. And keep an eye on him. Don't let him sneak up on me."

I have a million questions I want to ask Terrance. Like does the CIA know what I do? Who I am? Or about Black X?

"I've been doing some digging. There is nothing about your school anymore. It's like it didn't exist at all. And no one I've talked to has ever heard of Black X. There are, of course, black missions that are completely off the books, and there are rumblings of other double-black groups that do some of the CIA's dirty work, but not one named Black X. I also found out that when I went to Montrovia, I tenured my resignation to the CIA, citing a new job in the private sector."

"I'm going to be in town for at least a few days," I say randomly. "Then who knows where we'll decide to go. How about you?"

"Needless to say, the resignation was forged. I thought I was still working for the CIA. It stands to reason that I am now working for Black X, just like you."

"And did you win big at The Casino?"

"Yes, actually, it appears Black X pays quite handsomely. By direct deposit." I start to open my mouth to speak. He puts his hand up. "Before you ask, no. I tried, but couldn't trace where the money came from."

"I don't know. Maybe Paris," I reply randomly.

"The reason I brought you here is to tell you that I was able to access one of the files on the locket. It's a photo nearly identical to the one of the proposed Terra Project that was in Ophelia's home."

"What?" I say, not able to mask my response. I catch myself and start laughing, then punch Terrance in the shoulder. "You're silly," I say, rolling my eyes and flirting with him.

I look up and see Mike Burnes headed in our direction.

"Terrance, my boy," he says, laying his hand on

Terrance's shoulder. "How have you been?"

"Very well, thank you. Have you met Miss Von Allister?"

"We met at the bar. Good to see you again, Huntley. How do you two know each other?"

"We met in Montrovia," Terrance says at the same time I say, "We met at the Royal Casino."

I smile at Terrance and laugh. "We met at the Royal Casino in Montrovia. I was on a bit of a lucky streak at the roulette table. On a dare, Terrance asked if he could rub me for luck. It made me laugh, and we became instant friends."

"How lovely," he says.

"So how do you and Terrance know each other?" I ask, curious to hear his reply.

"Terrance is quite talented."

"I know! He's great with the computer! He managed to find me the vintage Chanel bag I have been searching for!" I act very excited.

The director actually looks surprised and gives Terrance a curious glance. "Well, isn't that great. Terrance helped me out doing something similar."

"Wow." I smile at Terrance. "Now, I'm really impressed."

"I just wanted to drop by and say hello. How is the new job going?"

"I definitely have more free time," Terrance replies

with a grin.

"Good to hear," he says.

Neither of us speaks until we watch him exit the building.

When Terrance starts to say something, I bug my eyes out then tap his shoulder in the exact spot the CIA director touched it.

"Excuse me," he says. "I'm going to use the men's room."

While he's gone, the waiter brings our drinks, appetizer, and dessert.

"Son of a bitch," Terrance says when he returns. "He put a bug on me. I left my suit jacket hanging in a stall. Alright, back to business. What does Ophelia's plan to end the monarchy in Montrovia have to do with your mother's death?"

"I don't know."

"Do you have any idea at all what the password might be?"

"No. She didn't tell me anything."

"Do you know what she was working on?"

"Honestly, I can't recall much of my past. It's like when she died, so did my memories."

"That can happen in Post Traumatic Stress Disorder. What did she tell you when she gave you the locket?"

"No, it couldn't be that easy." I jolt back in my seat, realization hitting me.

"What couldn't be that easy?"

"Did you try *Top Secret* as the password for the encryption?"

"No, why would—wait, that's what she told you?"

"Yes. Those were her exact words."

"That seems too easy," he says, "but I'll give it a whirl as soon as I'm somewhere secure."

"Are you on a new mission?"

"Actually, yes. I'm working with my hacker friend in Montrovia trying to track down the man who assassinated the President. I assume going after him will be your next mission."

"Are you making any progress?"

"Black X seems to know who the assassin is, but has no idea where he is. They also figured out how he was contacted when he took the hit. We're waiting to see if he is contacted again, and if not, we may try to lay a trap. The problem is we don't know his protocol and are afraid he would know it was a trap and then you would be in extreme danger." He smiles at me. "And we wouldn't want the girl who is all over the Internet carrying a patriotic handbag to the President's swearing in to be in danger."

"Shut up," I say, smacking him playfully and stealing the dessert.

WHEN I GET in my car, I open the envelope Terrance

shoved in my bag. The photo is nearly identical to the one found in Ophelia's home. I don't understand why my mom would have this photo or why it would be top secret.

My thought process is interrupted by a call from one of the Kates, letting me know she is on her way to my father's home and would like to speak with me in the study.

When I tell her Lorenzo's staff has taken over both the study and the dining room, she says, "Fine, your closet."

When I arrive, she's waiting for me with a stack of articles in hand.

"Your photo from the swearing in is in papers all over the world today. The tabloids are discussing your relationships with both King Vallenta and the First Son, and the fashion magazines are praising your attire. The dress and handbag you have on in this photo sold out of stores within minutes, and we're getting calls asking if you have an agent. This social media storm is not something we anticipated, but after much discussion, we have decided to go with it. All of this just continues to strengthen your cover."

"Kate, who do you work for?"

"The people who employ you."

"Do you know who that is? What their name is? Have you met them? Do you work with other agents?

How did you get hired? Who pays you?"

She looks down. "I'm afraid I'm not authorized to answer those questions."

"Do you actually know any of the answers to those questions?"

She shakes her head. "Not exactly. My father was a five-star general who was killed in the Pentagon on 9-11. When I was recruited, I was told my job would combine my degree and experience with helping the fight for our country. That's all I needed to know. And I'll admit, shopping for you and Ari has been a whole lot of fun. Since the swearing in, we've been working nonstop. We've created a website for you and hired a secretary to handle your calls. You've had numerous offers to appear on magazine covers and in advertisements. I'm told that you may be allowed to do some of these things."

"Told by who?"

"My boss."

"And how does your boss contact you?"

"Secure messaging. How do you feel about doing interviews?"

"I would prefer not to. Tell them I value my privacy."

"That will make them want you all the more."

"Kate, this is a dangerous game. What if someone figures out I'm not who I say I am?"

"They won't. I'm told your cover goes back to birth,

and your legend is fully legitimate."

"Still, I'm not ready for that kind of thing."

"Will you at least start posting some photos on your social media accounts once in a while? You've gone from a few hundred followers to four million since you went to Montrovia."

"Are you serious?"

"You're the new It girl, Huntley. You might as well embrace it."

ARI AND I enter the Domino Room at the Cafe Milagro in Georgetown from a side door. After seeing the Washington A-listers gathered inside, I'm shocked the streets aren't filled with paparazzi. In attendance are the host of a political news show, a famous choreographer, a former Secretary of State, a retired general whose memoirs are a best seller, a television network founder, a Super-Bowl-winning quarterback, and from the entertainment world, the trifecta of an Academy-award-winning actress, a Tony-award-winning actor, and members from a Grammy-winning-country band.

Sissy and Bill are wonderful hosts and introduce Ari and I to nearly everyone. I'm having a really enjoyable time.

Until the Director of the CIA makes a beeline toward me. "It's nice to see you again."

"It's nice to see you, as well. This is quite the gathering."

"Sissy is the ultimate hostess. I don't really do dinner parties, but I meet the most interesting mix of people at hers that I always try to attend. I was hoping to possibly speak to you in private."

"About what?"

"Why don't we step outside."

Merda. He knows.

"You have certainly come onto the scene fast," he says, repeating the same words Daniel said to me earlier in reference to why he didn't talk to me after the kidnapping. "I've been seeing your picture everywhere."

"I suppose when you inherit billions that's normal?" I shrug. "Not sure, it's my first time."

"Possibly, but it's not often that someone becomes so quickly entrenched with the rich and powerful set. How did you?"

"Oh, that's easy to answer. We got invited to a gala and were seated with Peter Prescott and his girlfriend, Allie, Daniel, and Senator and Mrs. Callan. We mentioned we were going to Montrovia for the race and, well, honestly, Allie sort of invited them to come with us. Then Daniel ended up coming to Montrovia, too."

"And did you meet the Prince through them?"

"Actually, no. Ari and I were shopping when Lorenzo decided on a whim to drop by his tailor's. He offered me his opinion on a tie I was picking out and then invited me to a party that night. I didn't go, though."

Mike Burnes has a genuine look of surprise on his face. "Why not?"

"We met this group of English lads at dinner who were a lot of fun. We ended up at The Casino, I got lucky playing roulette, and kind of forgot about it."

"I don't suppose the Prince was used to being stood up."

"It wasn't like a date. I assumed he invited numerous people to the party and wouldn't miss me in the least. Anyway, we made some new friends at The Casino and threw an impromptu party at our villa the next day. Daniel showed up with the Prince, and that's when he and I became friends."

"I understand you were with him during the attempts on his life."

"That was scary, but the kidnapping was—for lack of a better word, traumatic. I thought I was going to die."

"Your brother has an interesting background. Did you know he trained at a CIA facility but then dropped out?"

"Yeah, he told me. Not that it did us much good during the kidnapping, but whatever."

"It's possible you could help serve your country."

"And how would I do that?"

"By passing along information to us from time to time."

"You want me to be a snitch?"

"We prefer to call it an informant."

"Why me?"

"I was told by the British agent who rescued you that you were cool under pressure and had managed to get your hands untied. He thinks you're smart and resourceful."

"Did he also tell you that he bought me an expensive evening bag and tried to recruit me himself before we got kidnapped?"

"He did not."

"Of course, at that point, I thought his story of being a British agent was just a way to get in my pants."

The Director chuckles. "So will you be there if your country needs you?"

"I'm not sure. What would you want me to do? Like, give me an example."

"Say you are at the Royal Casino in Montrovia and there's a Russian billionaire who we think is moving arms to the bad guys."

"Like prosthetic arms?" I ask with a straight face, acting totally ditzy.

"Uh, what? Oh, no. I mean arms, like ammunition."

I giggle. "Oh, duh. Sorry. My brother was watching some show about this military guy who got his arm blown off and had this almost robotic one. That's the first thing that popped into my mind."

He studies me, and I can tell he's thinking I am an idiot. And quite honestly, I'd prefer him to think of me exactly that way.

"Anyway, he's a bad guy."

I nod, pretending to follow. "Got it."

"We want you to make friends with him, maybe let him buy you a drink."

"But I don't want to be friends with a bad guy."

"You would pretend."

"Oh, okay. Wait. Why would I do that?"

"Because we need time to search his car for clues."

"So, I'd be like a decoy. A distraction?"

"Yes. Exactly."

I make a little pouty face.

"Does that not sound like something you could do?"

"No, it does. I just thought it would be more exciting. Like I'd be searching for clues or something."

"Well, you could do that, too. If you were talking to the Russian and you overheard a clue, you'd want to tell us."

"This might be a stupid question, but why would I care if the guy is selling weapons? The CIA sells weapons."

"Maybe he's selling them to terrorists."

"What kind of weapons?"

"He dabbles in all kinds of things: RPGs, AKS-74Us, MG4s. Nasty stuff."

"Sounds serious, all those letters and numbers. I'm not sure someone like me would know what those things are."

"You wouldn't necessarily have to know—"

"Although, honestly," I interrupt, "if I were a terrorist, I'd probably be more interested in the L-85 assault rifle or maybe something like a RPK-12 light machine gun. Unless I really wanted to do some serious damage, then I might need an RPG-7 or a nice little Stinger rocket launcher."

"Were you playing dumb with me, before?"

"You were talking to me like I was, so I thought I would fulfill your wishes."

"How do you know what an L-85 assault rifle is?"

"Battleground," I say with a grin.

He rolls his eyes. "You kids and your damn video games."

"Can we try it now?"

"Try what now?"

"Point to someone and tell me what you want to know about them."

"Hmm." He scans the room and then gestures. "Over there is Senator Martin Vanderbilt. He's very protective of his family after a kidnapping scare a few years ago. He rarely speaks of them in public and would never give out any pertinent details. I want to know where his children are going to summer camp."

A FEW MINUTES later, I'm at the bar when the Director wanders over. "Ready to admit to defeat?"

"No, I was just grabbing a drink. His twelve-year old son, Austin, and his fourteen-year old daughter, Beatrice, are going to Lakeland Camp in the Adirondacks. Apparently, it's a family tradition. His college-aged son attended when he was younger and even served as a camp counselor. He also tried to set me up with said son, whose name is Nathaniel and who is very close by as he attends Georgetown Law School."

The man raises his eyebrow at me just slightly, showing a hint of surprise. "You did well. So, will you do it?"

"If it doesn't put me in danger," I shrug. "Sure, why not?"

"Good to hear. I actually have a mission for you."

"Um, okay?"

"This week the King is hosting a state dinner at the Montrovian Embassy. I'm told Aleksandr Nikolaevich may be in attendance."

"Is that Viktor's father?"

"Yes."

"And what does he have to do with anything?"

"There are rumors that his international shipping company may be smuggling arms to people we don't want to have them."

"I don't know about that, but the man sure builds a gorgeous yacht."

"Just keep your ears open, and if you hear anything of interest, call me directly," he says, then hands me a card with his cell number written on the back.

I take the card and put it in my clutch. I mean, it couldn't hurt to have the Director of the CIA on speed dial.

AFTER DINNER, I pull Ari aside. "The Director of the CIA just recruited me to be an informant. I suspect he will try to recruit you too."

"Do you think he knows the truth about us?"

"I don't think so."

"Which means our cover runs very deep." Ari eyes one of the members of the country band, a beautiful brunette, and says, "Which is a good thing. Now if you will excuse me, I have some hunting to do."

"Does that mean I should see myself home?"

"I'll let you know later, but I sure hope so."

I'M GETTING READY to text my driver when I hear Mike Burnes speaking in hushed tones on his phone as he's heading for the exit. I don't know why, but I follow him, watching as he rounds the corner and meets up with someone.

I keep my body flat against the building and then stealthily peek around the corner. Neither man is facing my direction but rather standing face-to-face, giving me a view of their profiles.

The man he's speaking to is tall and wearing a trench coat and hat, which is weird considering it's not cold or rainy out.

I move closer in an attempt to better hear their conversation, using a dumpster as cover.

I have no reason to be back here. It's dark, and smart young women don't walk down alleys alone at night.

"You're not going to like this," the man in the trench coat says. "We believe that the assassin known as The Priest made the hit on the President. There is no one else who could have done this."

"That's impossible. He's been dead since—"

"Since he was double-crossed and killed by whomever ordered the hit on one of our best agents and her daughter six years ago."

My ears perk up, and there's a burning sensation at the pit of my stomach. Is the agent he's talking about my mother?

"It's hard to believe we never found her daughter's body," the director says, shaking his head and looking sad. "I just pray whatever he did to her was over quickly." He pauses. "Hard to believe she'd be eighteen by now."

Are they talking about me? About my body? Do they think I'm dead? No, it can't be me. There must be another agent who was killed in that timeframe. Who had a daughter the same age as me.

The director continues. "What proof do you have that The Priest is alive?"

"There was a woman he was thought to be tied to. After some research, we discovered she was killed in a suspicious auto accident four years ago."

"What does that have to do with him if he was dead?"

"Exactly," the man states. "We believe the people who hired him found out he wasn't dead and attempted to rectify the situation."

"But no one knows for sure?"

"That's correct. He disappeared without a trace and more than likely altered his face. Facial recognition software has come up with nothing."

"Maybe he's living off grid?" the director suggests, although the way he says it isn't dismissive, more like he's playing devil's advocate.

"He had to get in our country somehow to do the hit."

"He could have been smuggled in."

"Something like that would require help from others. The Priest doesn't work that way. He never has."

"If he's truly alive, we need to find him before anyone else does. I want this played close to the vest. Get a team together. No more than four. And only those you trust explicitly. We can not allow this to leak until we know for sure."

"What will we do if we find him?"

"We take him out," the director says.

I realize they are finished with their conversation, and I need to get out of here quickly before they discover me. I manage to sneak back around the corner, but have only taken a couple steps when my foot collides with an empty can, making an audible noise.

I hear the sounds of feet hitting pavement behind me, so I take off running.

I can't get caught. I can't get caught.

I move as fast as I can back toward the entrance to the dinner party. Thankfully, no one is outside, so I barrel through the door and head straight for the ladies' room.

I lock myself in a stall and attempt to catch my breath.

Five minutes later, I text Ari.

Me: I'm feeling sick and want to go home. Should I go without you?
Ari: Where are you? I've been looking for you.
Me: Bathroom. Can you meet me out front?

He doesn't say anything when he sees me, just puts his arm around my shoulder and helps me in the car.

As he's driving away, he says, "What's wrong?"

"My mom worked for the CIA, and they think I'm

dead."

"What do you mean?"

I tell him what I overheard in the alley.

"And you think they were talking about you? It could have been anyone."

I shake my head and lay my hand across my belly, my gut knowing the truth. "They were talking about me."

"So what if they were. How does it affect you now?"

I tell him about the locket and what Terrance found on it. About how whatever my mom was working on at the time got her and my father killed.

"I had to study The Priest in school. They told us the folklore. Based on the jobs he managed to complete, he was the best. I wouldn't say I idolized him, because I don't think random killing for money is right, but there was a respect level."

"There's nothing wrong with that."

"Except that he killed my mother and if Terrance is right about our upcoming mission, we'll be sent to deal with him. It's what they've been training me for."

"If that's our mission, we'll complete it," he states confidently. But Ari hasn't studied him. Doesn't know what The Priest is capable of.

"I don't know if I'm ready," I reply softly.

ARI IS QUIET during the remainder of our drive home,

apparently thinking through this new discovery.

When we pull in the driveway he asks, "Why didn't they say anything about your dad? You said he was killed a few days later."

"I don't know. Maybe because he died differently?"

"Or he's still alive."

"No way. He was a good dad. He wouldn't have dumped me at Blackwood."

"What if it was for your own safety?"

I shake my head. "No. I don't believe that."

"You got out of the car," Ari disagrees. "What makes you think he didn't?"

"Because I watched the car blow up, and he wasn't out of it."

Ari purses his lips in thought and just nods.

LORENZO ISN'T HOME yet, so I go straight to my room and take a hot bath.

I need to calm down and think.

Ari's right.

Why does it matter if they think I'm dead? If the CIA doesn't know I'm still alive, I definitely work for a very powerful covert agency, who more than likely hid me away not only to train me, but possibly to keep me safe.

But safe from whom?
And why?

MISSION: DAY THREE

THE QUEEN OF Montrovia is having tea in the castle's parlor and reading the paper when a photo catches her eye, causing her to frown.

Huntley Von Allister, who had all of Montrovia thinking she might be their future Princess, is holding hands with Daniel Spear while his father is sworn in as President.

With a sigh, she picks up the phone and calls her son.

"Hello, Mother," he answers politely.

"Lorenzo, there is a matter that I need to discuss with you."

"Very well. Would you like to do so now?"

"Yes, I must. I fear you will not take the news well, however. Before your father passed, he issued a decree changing the date by which you must wed."

"Why didn't he tell me?"

"He liked Huntley and had hoped things would progress, so he gave it to me. He didn't want to put unnecessary pressure on your relationship. Speaking of which, where do things stand with you and Miss Von Allister?"

"Things are—complicated."

"By the fact that she is seeing another man? She is holding hands with Daniel Spear during his father's swearing in. Is it true that you are staying at her home in Washington?"

"Yes. It is."

"And where do you stand with her?"

"Mother, we have only just recently met. We then went through something traumatic. It may take some time for us to work through the, uh, details."

"So things will work between you?"

"I honestly don't know."

"Do you want it to?"

"Yes."

"Are you saying that you love her?"

"She is unlike any woman I have ever met before. Would you approve of her if I did?"

"I would need to get to know her better and, of course, there is the law to deal with. Your bride must be a citizen of Montrovia."

"Her citizenship is already in place."

"When did that happen? How did it happen?"

"I had it approved by the Prime Minister before the Queen's Ball and had planned to tell her once we were alone. I hoped it would be the first step in an official courtship."

"And that was interrupted by the kidnapping?"

"Yes, Mother."

"So what changed things?"

"I was nearly killed by my own cousin. Did that not shock you?"

"Nothing shocks me anymore," she says with a sigh, the years of being in the spotlight having taken their toll long ago.

"Not to mention Father's passing, the funeral, and the coronation."

"I was told you gave Huntley use of the Royal Yacht, and Daniel Spear accompanied her."

"That is correct. She had been seeing Daniel before we met. She thought that I didn't fancy her further."

"Why did she think that?"

"Because of how I behaved after the coronation. She thought we were over."

"You are the youngest King of Montrovia in the last hundred years and, unfortunately for you, your reputation proceeds you. You are seen in the public eye as a playboy who only cares about his personal pleasures.

When you were courting Miss Von Allister, that perception was starting to change, but the damage has not been repaired. The people need a King who they believe has their country's best interests at heart."

"And I will prove to them that I am worthy of their respect."

"You have two weeks to show progress with Miss Von Allister. If you are not together and publicly dating by the end of that time period, I will be forced to start arrangements for you to marry."

"Marry who?"

"Lady Elizabeth Palomar."

"Lizzie?"

"Yes. She comes from a good family, and her father seemed amiable to the idea."

"How would you know that already?"

"Your father spoke to him before he passed. He had planned to tell you, but then you started dating Huntley, so he told me to let it run its course before we brokered the deal."

"I am not in love with Lizzie."

"She is beautiful, and you will learn to love her just as I learned to love and respect your father. Of course, producing heirs will be of utmost importance and part of her duties as your wife."

He closes his eyes. "I won't allow it."

"I'm afraid you don't have much choice, Lorenzo.

The decree your father signed proclaimed you must marry by your twenty-fourth birthday. You have two options. Get engaged to the woman of your choosing, or you will be betrothed to Elizabeth."

MY SLEEP IS fitful and filled with crazy dreams. I wake up starving and have breakfast sent to my room.

I'm just finishing up when there is a soft knock on my door, and Lorenzo whispers, "Are you awake?"

"Yes, come in," I reply.

"Did you sleep well?" he asks, sitting on the edge of my bed.

I push my tray away and pretzel my legs. "Not really. Did you?"

"It is hard for me to get much sleep when I am in such close proximity to you."

I wink at him. "Dirty dreams?"

"Yes, the kind where our chess game wasn't halted."

I smile. "If it's any consolation, telling you no that night was very difficult for me."

"That is good to know," he beams. "This morning, I am meeting with business and government leaders to discuss the worldwide terror crisis. Then I'll be touring some of the Washington monuments this afternoon. Would you care to join me?"

"I would love that. What time shall I be ready?"

"Around two o'clock? We'll have a private tour of the

Library of Congress and then go to the National Archives. I decided to have a monument built in honor of my father and thought those would provide some inspiration."

I take his hand in mine and give it a little squeeze. "Lorenzo, that's such a sweet idea. What kind of monument?"

"Much like you, my father loved history. I thought either a museum or library, where we could house much of Montrovia's history for the public to see. Right now, they get glimpses of history during the castle tour, but after the attack, it's been advised that I close the grounds to tourists."

"It's sad, really. That people can't just get along."

"It is," he agrees. "But the world has changed since I was a boy. Someday in the near future, I hope to have children of my own running around. My family's safety would be of the utmost importance. This would be a good compromise."

I reach out and touch his face. "You are going to be an amazing King. Do you know that?"

"History will be the judge of that."

"Then I hope I am around to watch your history unfold."

"You could be," he says. "In fact, if you play your chess pieces right, you could end up by my side, history unfolding for both of us together."

"If we stay friends, which I hope we do, I will be."

"That's not what I meant, and you know it."

I tilt my head. "I'm trying to avoid that topic. There isn't much more to say on the matter."

"That is where you are wrong, my dear. You merely won a battle, not the entire war."

I laugh. "Regardless, I like your idea of a monument for your father."

He glances at his watch. "I must leave, but will be back here at two to pick you up. We'll have dinner and then do a nighttime tour of the monuments. I'm told they are beautiful at night."

"That sounds wonderful," I tell him as he gives me a kiss and departs.

I WORK OUT with Ari in the house's gym. He's well-trained in boxing and martial arts, and it's fun to spar with him.

"I wish we could go to a shooting range. I used to practice every day, and it seems weird not to. But I don't know what the public would think of Huntley Von Allister going to one."

"Probably depends what kind of designer handbag you'd carry there," he teases.

"Very funny." I grip his arm and whip him over my shoulder onto the mat.

"You're in luck. Did you notice the spiral staircase

over there?" he asks, still sprawled flat out on his back.

"Yes."

"It will take you below the room we are in now, which houses a three-lane bowling alley, a basketball court, and a shooting range."

"Really? Can we go down there now?"

"Yeah, sure. Come on."

I follow him down the staircase, past the bowling lanes and the court to another door with a keypad. Ari says, "The code for all the doors in the house is 032872."

"This is fantastic," I say, looking in.

"It is," Ari agrees, moving toward the gun case, where there is a wide variety, from pistols, to rifles, to assault weapons.

"If the house is ever under attack, we know where to go," I tease.

"Why do you think he has a gun range in the basement?" Ari asks. "To me, that's a little odd."

"He worked on military stuff. Was Ares ever in the military himself?"

"No, but his father was a Marine. Maybe he taught him to shoot."

"Probably. My dad did."

"So did mine," Ari says, choosing a military grade black Glock G30.

"Oh, I want to shoot this one." I pick up a limited edition Sig Sauer P220. "Isn't it pretty?"

"Guns aren't supposed to be pretty. They're supposed to be lethal."

"That doesn't mean you can't appreciate the beauty of this one. Five-inch barrel, lightweight alloy beavertail frame, anodized finish, adjustable target sights, and the rosewood handle is so supple. Shall we have a little contest? See which of us is best?"

"Absolutely," Ari says, clipping on a target and sending it back.

We grab the proper ammunition, put on our headphones, and shoot.

When the targets are pulled back in, Ari looks at the tight circles and says, "You're better than I thought."

I punch him. "Gee, thanks."

AFTER SPENDING A few hours shooting a multitude of different firearms, my phone buzzes.

"Terrance is on his way over. He got into my mom's locket."

"Let's have him meet us down here. I scanned this room for surveillance devices and found none."

"What about the rest of the house?"

"Clean as far as I can tell," he says, which I find interesting as I run upstairs to greet Terrance.

ONCE WE'RE ALL in the range, Terrance takes out a small device and does another scan, just to be sure.

"I feel comfortable talking here now," Terrance says. "Huntley, you were right. The passcode was *Top Secret.* I entered it, and everything opened."

"And?" I ask hopefully.

"There's a lot of information to go through, and I haven't had the chance to do that yet, just gave it a cursory glance, but I have to tell you, what I'm seeing doesn't make a lot of sense. I think it was just a junk file."

He pulls up a photo of the Terra Project. "This looks similar to the one found in Ophelia's house, but the only indication of its location is the sand that surrounds it. So, if the Terra project is what got your mom killed, although I highly doubt it since it's a peaceful initiative, she must have been to a site where one was actually built. A quick computer search didn't tell me where that might be."

"What else?"

"That's where it gets a little strange. The rest is nothing but a bunch of conspiracy theories."

"Conspiracy theories? Like what?" Ari asks.

"Like we're being poisoned with fluoride in our water. That genetically modified foods are destroying our immune systems. There's information in here about chemical trails, crop circles, and terrorist attacks all being done by those who want to make the world one country. A new world order. I don't understand why she'd bother to save this information. It's not like you can't find all of it on the Internet."

"Unless she had proof those things were true. Did you see any proof?"

"No, I didn't. The only other thing on there were some random vacation photos. I'll have them printed out for you. I really don't think the disc has anything to do with how your mom died. I think she just wanted you to have the memories."

"Thanks for trying, Terrance," I say, holding back tears. "At least now we know."

AT PRECISELY TWO in the afternoon, Lorenzo arrives back at the house.

"Don't you look lovely?" He takes in the Dolce & Gabbana lemon print dress I'm wearing along with low-heeled black zip-up booties and matching lemon print handbag. I have a supple black leather jacket thrown over my arm since it will be cooler this evening.

I give him a wide grin, quite possibly melting a little.

HE ESCORTS ME to the limo, and we spend the first hour taking in the architecture at the Library of Congress.

"I think your father's monument is going to be quite expensive if you want it to look anything like this," I tell him.

"It's interesting how new your country is," Lorenzo

states.

"In Europe, I'm always amazed at how old everything is. Like your castle. Do you ever wish it were more modern?"

"Although my penthouse in New York City is quite modern, most of my other homes have a lot of old world charm. It's what I feel comfortable in."

"Because it reminds you of home?"

He nods. "What was your home like, growing up?"

"We lived a lot of different places. Traveled all over. But I loved the home we lived in, you know, when it happened."

"What style was it?"

"Cape Cod. It had worn wood floors, shutters, and felt a touch nautical."

"My mother informed me that she'd like to move into my Uncle's home since it is empty. She thinks I will need the castle to myself for my future family."

"And you told her that she is your family, right?"

He smiles at me. "You are right. I also suggested that she build a cottage on the palace grounds instead."

"Why does she want to move now? It's not like you're getting married soon."

He grimaces slightly but hides it quickly. "She says she needs a fresh start."

"But you think it's too soon?"

"It's only been a short time since my father passed.

She shouldn't be making decisions right now."

"Give her some time. I'm sure she'll come around to your way of thinking. She loves you and wants to make you happy."

He takes my hand and presses his lips against it. "As I do you."

I want to ask him to clarify that. I'm sure he meant he wants to make me happy, not that he loves me. But just as I'm about to open my mouth, Juan interrupts the moment to tell us our car is waiting out front.

UPON ARRIVAL TO the Archives, we are escorted through a back entrance. We're getting a VIP tour that allows us to see the preservation rooms as well as some of the pieces that are rotated on and off display. It's cool to see the care that is given to our country's important documents.

Next, we are taken to the grand hall where the Declaration of Independence is displayed. The place is packed with summer vacationers and full of children.

"There it is," Lorenzo says. "Your Declaration of Independence. It's incredible to think that a new country, your government, was created by a few men with great foresight."

"America has become a super power in a very short time. Do you think it will be like other world powers who have fallen, or will it be able to maintain this status?"

"If history is any indication, all super powers eventually fall. My father always said we should learn from the mistakes of the past. And we can learn much from the history of our countries. Montrovia is like Switzerland. We remain neutral in world politics. It keeps us from getting involved in costly wars."

"That's true, but terror has yet to come to your country."

"And it probably will not because we've created no animosity with any country."

"You flaunt your wealth and western ways, isn't that enough for some?"

"Perhaps," he agrees, "but the deep seeded hate is not there."

"I wish there was no hate in the world," I say with a sigh, then point to the document and change the subject. "Did you know there's an invisible map on the back of it?"

He smiles. "I've seen that movie." He wraps an arm around my shoulder, pulling me close enough so that he can whisper in my ear. "I think in another life I was a treasure hunter. So much excitement. Speaking of that, you've been spending time with me. I like it but was wondering, am I still your mission?"

I shake my head. "No, you are not."

"So you are here with me simply because you enjoy

my company?"

"Yes," I say, standing on my tiptoes and kissing his cheek. "I most certainly am."

He's pulling me in for a kiss when my peripheral vision notices something out of place.

Shit. We have to act quickly.

I duck behind Lorenzo's shoulder and tap Juan. "Three o'clock. Black puffy jacket."

"It's not cold out," he says.

"And there are a lot of children and families here. We have to do something."

Nearly everyone in the place is taking photos and videos. If I tried to approach the man, it could end horrifically, not to mention completely blow my cover. But that would be better than being blown to bits.

Juan reaches for his concealed weapon.

"Don't do that! If he has a bomb, you'll risk him setting it off and killing everyone in here. Including us."

"Well, what would you suggest?" he says sarcastically.

"If you want to play the hero, you can hug him tightly, which would lessen the bomb's impact. You would die but you'd save a lot of people."

"Any other brilliant ideas?"

"You need to go behind the bomber, grab him around the shins, lift up, and push forward. He should instinctively put his hands out to break his fall. Once his hands are away from the bomb's trigger, shove your knee into his back to keep him down flat. Then you can shoot him if need be."

The other guards surround Lorenzo and I, but I'm not sure why they are bothering. If the man does have a bomb, and it goes off, it won't matter. We'll all be dead.

Juan circles behind the man.

"Lorenzo," I whisper. "You need to leave the building."

"Maybe the man is just chilly?"

"He's here by himself, wearing a coat in the middle of summer, and his lips are moving."

"Then we need to stay here and help these people. Are you armed?"

"Actually, I am, but if I shoot him, the bomb could still explode. Let's see if Juan can handle it."

I wait until Juan dives into the man's shins then yell out, "He's got a bomb! Everyone get out!"

A mass panic occurs, people scream and run for their lives.

This helps to clear the area around the bomber. Juan jabs his knee in the man's back, but the man keeps struggling.

I'm afraid he will get free.

No one is looking at me, so I shoot the man in the neck with a tranquilizer dart, causing him to quickly stop struggling as he goes limp.

Juan narrows his eyes at me then rolls the man over

and opens his jacket.

"There is no bomb," he says. "Merda."

"Check his underwear," I say. "I read in the paper the other day that—"

"I'm not unzipping his pants," Juan argues. "If you're wrong about this, it's going to be a social media nightmare."

I bend down and unzip the unconscious man's pants, proving my point.

"Holy mother, will you look at that?"

"I've heard about those," one of the other guards says. "They use liquid explosives, like TATP and nitroglycerin. We only had to go through a magnetometer here. It wouldn't have picked it up."

"Get your hands in the air!" a policeman yells as we are surrounded by lots of men with guns.

"Drop the weapon," another yells at Juan.

"I am the King of Montrovia," Lorenzo says, his voice booming as he steps directly into their line of fire. "These men are part of my security detail. Because of their quick thinking, they took down a suicide bomber who nearly caused the deaths of many people. Lower your guns and treat them with the respect they deserve."

To my surprise, the men do exactly as told.

I can't help but smile with pride.

AN HOUR AND a million questions later, we are allowed

to leave.

The good news is they don't believe the man was targeting Lorenzo. The bad news is he got past their security.

"I think we should skip the rest of our tour," Juan says.

WHEN WE GET back to the house, Juan asks to speak to me in private.

"Miss Von Allister," he says formally. Usually he calls me Huntley. "May I ask why you have a watch that shoots tranquilizer darts? Darts that look much like the ones used when you, your brother, and the Prince were kidnapped?"

I look down at my watch, wondering what I could tell him to allow me to maintain my cover.

I slump my shoulders and sigh, like I'm about to tell him a secret.

"As one would expect, being kidnapped kind of freaked my brother and I out. I suggested getting a gun for protection, but Ari said that I would end up shooting myself. So we did some research and found a website with all these covert, spy-type gadgets." I hold my arm up, showing him the watch. "With their help, we retrofitted this watch to hold two tranquilizer darts."

"Okay, let's say I buy that," he says, scrutinizing me. "How is it that you knew the proper way to take down a suicide bomber?"

I look him straight in the eye and lie through my teeth. "Ari and I worked with a professional security advisor. Although we are not royalty, we're told that our money could make us a target, particularly for kidnapping. So we were taught some basic techniques. That was one of them. I was really impressed with how well it worked."

"I can't believe I listened to you," he says with a smile, shaking his head. I'm not sure he totally buys it, but at least he goes along with my story. "However, I'm glad I did. Can you give me the name of the firm? I think I'd like to have them do a training session for the King's guards."

"Um." Merda. "Absolutely, I'll have Ari get you his name. We considered hiring our own security guards, but that seemed a bit pretentious. Ari and I aren't used to all this media attention. I suppose Lorenzo grew up with it and doesn't know anything different."

"He did, and he often acted out accordingly," Juan says with a laugh. "You're good for him. After the kidnapping, he distanced himself from you."

"I know. He wouldn't talk to me."

"But he wanted you to attend his coronation."

"To get back the Royal Jewels, I assumed."

"His sending you on the boat and not going with you was a mistake on his part."

"Juan, I'm not sure I could handle the pressures of being a princess, let alone be the queen of your country."

"And I'm thinking you most certainly could. You're unflappable, smart, and quick on your feet. Because of you, we're all alive."

"Is it just me, or does the King's security team seem a little, um, old?"

"I suggested that he offer his father's guards nice retirement packages and recruit his own men. He declined."

"Maybe after today, you should remind him of that."

He smiles. "Maybe you should be the one to tell him."

I nod in agreement. "I think I will."

LORENZO IS IN the study taking calls from reporters. I sit down in one of the chairs not already occupied by his staff.

When he finishes the call, his personal secretary says, "CNN wants you in studio tonight to talk about the events of today, the other attempts on your life, and your new role as King."

His eyes meet mine, and he smiles. "Tell them I have other plans for this evening."

"What about first thing in the morning?" she counters.

"Tomorrow is the funeral for the President," he

reminds her.

She looks frustrated. "Very well then."

"I'm done for the day," Lorenzo states, then he walks over, takes my hand, and pulls me out of my seat. "We aren't going to let this ruin our evening. And we're going out alone." He addresses his staff. "I want you all to take the night off. Go enjoy the city."

Although they protest, they don't put up a fight. Soon we're in the study alone.

I shut the doors and fix Lorenzo a drink.

"Can I talk to you about today? Not only as someone who cares for you, but also to give you my professional opinion?"

"Certainly."

"You need a new security detail. The men who guarded your father are out of shape, slow to react, and not up to date with current threats in the world. They should have constant training, not rest on their laurels. You should promote Juan and let him recruit the best of the best from the Montrovian Special Forces. Guarding you may be an honor, but it's more than that."

He sets his drink down and slips his arm around my waist. "Or I could marry you."

"If I marry you, I will lose my abilities, as well. Something I'm not prepared to do."

"What if I hired you as my *very* personal body guard?" he asks, his eyes smoldering. "A man of my position would most definitely require constant care. Particularly at night, in my bed."

"You are not taking me seriously."

"Oh, but that is where you are wrong. I would take having you in my bed extremely seriously."

"I mean about your guard."

"I'm glad you are worried about my safety, and you are probably right. I'll talk to Juan about it tomorrow, and he can start the process." He kisses me, sending shivers down to my toes. "Back to you in my bed."

"I thought you wanted me in your limo so we could take in the monuments at night?"

He narrows his eyes at me.

"I want you in my limo, alright."

"Lorenzo!" I screech.

"But, Huntley, my dear, I am very serious about it. You may have to fight me off."

I raise an eyebrow at him. "Challenge accepted."

"Merda," he mutters. "How am I ever supposed to have my way with you when you so easily can fend off my advances?"

"If I want things to advance, I am certainly capable of letting you know."

"And how will you do that?" he asks with a smirk. "Can you give me details?"

"Go get in the limo before you get yourself in trouble." I laugh.

MISSION: DAY FOUR

ALTHOUGH DANIEL TEXTED me late last night and asked me to attend the funeral with him, it was vetoed by his family this morning, who said that a solemn occasion such as this should not be made a media spectacle like what happened with the swearing in photo.

And I guess I can respect that.

It made it easier for me, since Lorenzo also requested that I accompany him. Ari could have come with us but decided there was no need.

"The man's dead, there's nothing further we can do for him," he says callously as Lorenzo and I are leaving. His words make Lorenzo flinch, but I suspect his harshness comes more from his personal losses than from a lack of respect.

When we arrive at the National Cathedral, a media

spectacle is already taking place. Thousands are lined up on the streets waving American flags along the hearse's route to the funeral. Reporters from every station—from local to international—seem to be present. And although there is no red carpet, there might as well be with all the recognizable faces. Republicans, Democrats, world leaders, former Presidents, political dignitaries, and celebrities, all dressed in black, come together to mourn for our nation.

And although I am here to do the same, I have another job. I want to scan the crowd looking for someone who seems out of place. Someone whose calculating eyes betray their feelings. Someone who isn't sad, but rather who may have benefited from the President's death.

But the only person I can see who has directly benefited is Daniel's father, and he is visibly upset, particularly when the flag-draped casket is carried down the aisle by a military honor guard and placed at the front of the church.

WHEN THE FUNERAL is over the casket is taken out of the church, followed by the former President's family.

Lorenzo leans over and whispers to me, "The casket and family will be taken on Air Force One to President Hillford's home state of Massachusetts, where he will be buried on the grounds of what will be his Presidential Library."

I expect to be let out of the church row by row, but once the family and casket, along with the current President and his family—including Daniel who looked devilishly handsome in a dark suit and who gave me a wink as he walked by—are out of the church, everyone gets up and mingles. People are being comforted by one and other. Hugs, greetings from people who haven't seen each other in "ages," and even an occasional peel of laughter—the sounds of the living fill the air.

While Lorenzo is making his rounds, I stand by his side looking pretty and using the time to survey the crowd. I haven't spotted anyone rubbing their hands together like the evil men on cartoons, happy their nefarious plan has come together—if only it were that easy.

"Huntley, I'd like you to meet Malcolm Prescott, Peter's father," Lorenzo says, introducing me to a distinguished looking man wearing a very expensive Italian suit.

"It's a joy to finally meet you," he says. "Peter has told me much about you. What an interesting story you have. Is your brother here with you? Ares and I were quite close. I never knew he had children." He studies my face then smiles at me. "But it's obvious you are his daughter. You have his eyes."

"How did you know each other?" I ask.

"We were friends back when we all thought we were

at the top of our game, having each earned our first million before we were twenty-five." He smiles a sad smile. "Except for the man we laid to rest here today. He simply turned twenty and received a large trust fund. But it was that trust fund that gave the three of us, who had nothing to speak of, the seed money for the businesses we went on to create."

"So you, President Hillford, and my father were friends?"

"Yes, along with Aleksandr Nikolaevich. I believe you met his son, Viktor, in Montrovia." He smiles at me. "Your father was obsessed with racing, not to mention all sorts of other fun gadgets. Through him we were invited by Ferrari to attend the Montrovian Grand Prix." He turns toward Lorenzo. "Which is where we met your father when he was still a prince." He gives Lorenzo a little slap on the back. "And from what I've heard, you are a chip off the old block. Your father was quite the ladies' man."

Lorenzo almost chokes. "Really?"

"Yes, but as men eventually do, he settled down. Except for Ares," he says to me. "He told us he would never let a woman tie him down. How did you come to find out you are his children?"

"Apparently a woman never did tie him down, because Ares was never in our lives. An attorney contacted us both. Quite frankly, I didn't really believe it. I thought I was being punked. I was half expecting someone to jump out from behind a door, laugh at me, and send me on my way with a toaster oven for being a good sport."

"What evidence did they show you that changed your mind?"

"My brother," I say with a smile. "When we were introduced, it was"—I make myself tear up—"overwhelming, I guess." I fan my face in an attempt to keep the tears from falling. "And one look at him and I knew it was true. And it's cool, because neither of us have any family."

"Your father's estate holds a large amount of my company's stock, and I still am heavily invested in Von Allister Industries. That sort of makes *us* like family." He pats my back in comfort. "My wife is famous for her social gatherings. As a matter of fact, we're having a soiree at our home in London starting on Sunday with festivities before the Cartier Queen's Cup, and then throughout the week before and after the Royal Ascot. Peter and his new friend—what is her name?"

"Allie."

"Ah, yes. The apple doesn't fall far from the tree. I am afraid I can't keep track of my son's women. Peter and Allie are already in London, and we would love for the three of you to join us."

"I was planning on attending both events," Lorenzo

says. "We'd love to."

"It was very nice to meet you, Huntley," he says.

"You, as well. Maybe in London you could tell me more about Ares? His life sounds, um, rather complicated, the last years of his life. It would be nice to know what he was like before that."

"I will look forward to it." He shakes Lorenzo's hand and kisses my cheeks.

"He's really nice," I say to Lorenzo after he walks away. "Reminds me of Peter. Easy to get to know but without the pompous ass factor."

"I suppose it's because he didn't grow up with wealth as Peter has. He had to work for it." Lorenzo glances at his watch. "I need to say hello to the Prince of Denmark, then we can make our departure. I'm due back for a conference call with the Prime Minister shortly."

"I'm going to run and find a restroom. I'll meet you back here," I reply, happily. Earlier I saw someone I'd like to talk to.

I'm halfway to the bathroom when Gallagher finds me.

"Huntley Von Allister, how lovely to see you again," he says formally.

"What are you doing here?"

"Paying my respects, of course," he says, but then lowers his voice. "I was hoping to see you."

"Aww, did you miss me?"

"I most certainly did." He hands me a business card with the name and address of a designer shoe store. "And in case you'd like to go shopping for another handbag, I'd highly recommend this place."

"Are you buying again?"

He smiles, kisses my cheeks, and moves away, effortlessly disappearing into the crowd.

I slide the card into my clutch and then reunite with Lorenzo.

Once we're in the limo, and Lorenzo is busy on the phone, I slip the card out and flip it over. On the back, written in neat print is a time. One that is a few hours away.

AT THE HOUSE, I tell Lorenzo that I'm going shopping and will be back in time for the dinner tonight. When I go to the garage to pick a car to drive, I find Terrance and Ari deep in discussion.

"What's going on?"

"We should receive details of our mission sometime in the next forty-eight hours, so we need to be ready," Ari says.

"Ready for what?" I ask.

"The assassin was contracted for not just one hit, but a series of them," Terrance expands. "Our hacker learned how the assassin was contacted. We can't retrieve past communication, so we're waiting to receive the next hit location. Your mission will be to track the assassin and find out who hired him."

"So you don't want us to interfere with the second hit?"

"If you can stop the assassination without alerting him to your presence, that is fine. But following him is your primary concern. You can't risk losing him."

"If we're going to follow him, we'll need disguises. He didn't get to be the best without being really good at his job. If he even thinks he's being followed, he'll be gone."

"Tell me what you need," Terrance says.

I give him a list, explain how I want it all arranged, and the exact look of the backpack I want.

"What about weapons?" Ari asks.

"That's where things get tricky," Terrance says. "We expect that the second hit will take place here in the United States, since we have no indication that he has left the country. But depending on where he has to go next, travel—possibly international travel—could be involved. We have to be prepared for that. This will be a particularly dangerous mission that will be conducted on the fly, so our job will be monitoring and supporting you."

"*Our* job?" I ask Terrance.

"Remember the hacker friend I told you about in Montrovia?"

"What's his name?"

"*Her* name is Olivia but in her world, she's known as Plague. She can wipe out anything."

"But you've been referring to her as a him."

"The Plague is believed to be male. It's part of her online persona."

"Very creative," Ari says, not impressed.

Terrance's eyes light up. "I know, right? She is amazing. Seriously. I've never seen anyone do what she can. Her parents were MIT professors, and I'm pretty sure she learned computer code before she could speak."

"Sounds like you have a crush," Ari states, raising an eyebrow.

Terrance blushes. "Oh, no. We have a strictly working relationship."

"Okay," he says, not really believing him.

"Anything else I need to know?" I ask.

"Yes, besides the things you requested, I'll be prepping our communication and surveillance system. We will be live with you during this mission. We will be able to see what you see and communicate with you."

"So we're the drones, and you're going to fly us from your safe little cave?"

"No," Terrance says, slightly offended. "Our job is to help and support you. Try to relax and mentally prepare yourself."

"Which I will be doing by going shopping. I just

came to get a car."

"Which one are you taking?" Ari asks.

I point at my favorite. "She's mine now, in case you were wondering."

"Oh, a little sibling rivalry," Terrance teases as I get in the car and take off.

I stop at the estate's gate, taking a moment to enter the address for the shopping center, rather than the specific store, into the navigation map on my phone. I see that it's not far away and realize I still have some time to kill.

And I know exactly where I want to go.
Blackwood Academy.

I TAKE A circuitous route to the school, making sure I'm not being followed. As an extra precaution, I take the SIM card out of my phone and shut it off, then proceed to the place I called home for last six years.

I feel a little giddy when the stately mansion comes into view. I'm excited to see everyone. To find out what they will do after graduation. Who they will be working for, what missions they will be going on. If we will get to work together.

Mostly, I'm excited to see M.

The first thing I notice as I approach the school is that there are no cars anywhere to be seen.

Prickles run down my spine.

Something feels off.

I quickly change plans, based on my gut feeling, and drive by the school without stopping. I continue up the little used road for a mile or so, then flip around in a driveway, pretending to be lost.

As I pass the school again, I don't even glance in its direction. Instead, I go down the road a quarter mile and turn left onto a gravel road, silently praying to the Ferrari gods to forgive me. I drive for another quarter mile, park the car so it's hidden in a thicket of trees off school grounds, then get out and make my way down a path I know well.

This is how M and I used to sneak out to go dancing.

When I get to the fence that surrounds the grounds, I stay hidden in the trees, searching for any sign of activity. I notice the cameras that used to be fixed on the fence are gone. In fact, all the cameras that used to be on the buildings are gone, as well.

I slow my breathing and then make my move, running from the tree I was hiding behind, to the break in the fence, and then across the property to the out building that houses both the gym and the gun range.

The sound of a twig snapping causes me to flatten myself against the wall.

I don't dare move.

I hear the noise again and chastise myself for not bringing a weapon.

The noise gets closer, and I know I have to make my move. I leap out from behind the building, ready to take on whoever is there.

Instead, there are two deer, a mother and her fawn, happily grazing on the lush grass.

I let out a sigh of relief.

But the deer cause me the same concern as the lack of vehicles. If people were around, the deer wouldn't be.

I run to the back door of the range and find it unlocked.

When I get inside, my mouth falls opens in shock.

The building is empty.

Totally and completely empty. There's not even a speck of dust on the floor.

It's then that I realize I'm not wearing gloves. That my fingerprints are on the handle of the door.

I pull the sleeve of my cardigan over my hands and carefully wipe down the door handle while my mind is going a million miles an hour trying to figure out what's going on.

Terrance told me they were closing the school, but I didn't expect it to be so soon. I decide to go into the main building. Maybe they just cleaned the out buildings in prep for the closure. Maybe everyone is inside, hanging in their dorm rooms waiting for graduation to start.

Or maybe they changed the time and it's tonight

instead of this afternoon. Or maybe they moved the ceremony to a different location. Although if they had, wouldn't the Dean have mentioned it?

Or did he not want me to come?

No, that's silly. Why would he care? Everyone at graduation knows who I am and probably now knows my cover. M was obsessed with tabloids. She'd for sure have seen me with Lorenzo in them.

I wonder what she thought.

She would have loved everything about it except for the fact that I'll probably end up behind some desk in a basement because of it. She always joked and said we were too pretty for that.

She could always make me laugh—usually at totally inappropriate times that ended up getting us both reprimanded.

I consider going in the front door, but my goose-bumps and the weird feeling in my gut lead me to sneak around the back of the house and go through the kitchen entrance. We used to joke that when something bad was about to go down our *Spidey-senses* would kick into gear.

That's how I feel right now. My Spidey-senses are on full alert.

I can't shake the feeling that something is wrong here.

And what I see when I step inside doesn't help me feel better.

The kitchen is empty.

And all of a sudden, I don't feel alone, even though the place seems to be deserted.

I move quickly and silently through the kitchen then to the front entry, past the Dean's empty office, and up the grand staircase. I slide my sleeve down the thick, polished chair rail like I always used to and make my way to my dorm room.

Everything is gone.

I don't understand how this is possible. Where did everyone go? Where is all my stuff?

I stand in front of my window that looks out over the treed property feeling sad. It's like going back home to find your parents moved out and left you.

Most everything of importance I had was in the backpack I always carried with me. It was something my mom taught me—*If you have to leave on a moment's notice, always have a bag packed and ready to go.*

But I kept a journal under my mattress. I had some books and a few trinkets. What I don't have is the key to my parents' safety deposit box.

I guess it's time to find out just how thorough they were.

I step into my closet, stretch up high, and run my fingers across the top of the door jamb until they connect with a metal object—my key.

Feeling relieved, I slip the key into my pocket and

decide there's really no reason for me to stay here any longer. I take one last look out the window and am turning around when I hear a creak from the hallway.

I quickly assess my options. I'm on the second story with a bank of three windows offering an exit onto the porch roof. It wouldn't be the first time I'd gone out that way. I could risk going into the hall, but that would be bad from a tactical standpoint. Anyone out there could pick me off the second I peeked through the door. The closet would offer cover, but I would be trapped—which is never good.

I consider opening the window, but know that can't be done quietly. When I hear another creak, this time closer, I move into the closet and flatten myself against the wall. At least if someone steps inside, I will have a brief moment of surprise. There's a good chance whoever is out there doesn't know which room I am in.

A few more creaks tell me a person has entered the room. The shadow of a hooded figure carrying a gun moves across the wall.

When the figure steps into the closet, I attack, grabbing their gun arm and rotating it in a circle, stopping just short of breaking it when the gun falls from their hand. I quickly follow that with a palm to the chin. The assailant lunges forward, wrapping his arms around my waist and pushing me into the closet wall with a thud.

I head butt him, smashing into his nose. His hands

react naturally, flying toward his face as I dive for the gun.

I grab it then tuck and roll, spinning so that I'm in a shooting position in one fluid movement.

Then I take aim.

"Jeez, X, you about broke my nose," the hooded man says in a voice I recognize.

"Josh?! What are you doing? Why did you just attack me?"

"Because I don't know whose side you're on."

"What are you talking about?"

He pulls his hoodie sleeve down and uses it to stop the bleeding.

"Tell me why you left school when you did!"

"Why does that matter?"

"It does, okay?! Answer the freaking question!"

"I was sent on a mission."

"Why are you here now?"

"Because today is graduation day. Where is everyone?"

"They changed graduation to yesterday," he says, looking visibly shaken.

"Josh, what's wrong?"

He takes a deep breath and lowers his hands away from his face. "This year's graduation included a reunion of all former students and faculty."

"I bet that was fun, seeing everyone."

"It wasn't fun, X. They're all dead. Everyone. Gunmen came in. They had assault rifles."

"What about M?"

"She was giving a speech and was one of the first killed."

"Oh my god. And the Dean?"

"He wasn't in attendance. Professor Gunner was doing the ceremony. What you aren't understanding is that I got away. I'm the *only* one who got away. Thirty-three dead and there's nothing about it on the news. Don't you find that a bit odd? Where are their families?"

"Where is your family?"

"Dead," he says. "Probably true of all the students, now that I think about it. It's obvious that we were all disposable, but why would someone take the time and effort to train us, only to kill everyone?"

"They wouldn't do that, Josh. It doesn't make sense. You're not making sense."

"That's why I fell for you. Even though you are serious, smart, and have a tough veneer, there's an underlying vulnerability to you."

"No, there's not."

He reaches his hand out to help me up. I accept his hand but still keep my revolver trained on him.

"Yeah, there is," he says. "When you get tired, it shows in your eyes. And when you sleep, you have bad dreams. X, I need to know. Was what we had real, or did you sleep with me because you thought I was your best shot of getting the flag?"

"We didn't even know there was going to be a mission enactment."

"We knew one was coming."

"What does any of that have to do with what happened?"

"I hid in the woods until nightfall hoping the authorities would come. But then I was afraid if they did and found me, they might think I did it. So I left and spent most of the night in a truck stop. It was there that I saw a photo of you on the cover of a tabloid. I was shocked. All your covert training and you're on the cover of a magazine? It didn't make sense, so I did a little more digging. I learned that *apparently* you're the long lost daughter of a reclusive billionaire. That you were recently in Montrovia and caught the attention of their Prince. Then I read about your kidnapping and how you were saved by a British Intelligence agent. I suspect that's all propaganda. You left school and were sent on a mission to protect the Prince, right?" He doesn't give me a chance to reply; he keeps speaking. "We were all trained to move in the circles of the rich and powerful, but not out in the open. Not like you are. Why train you to be covert only to blow your cover immediately? But then I saw that you were in Washington for the State Funeral, and that's when it clicked."

"What clicked?"

"Were you sent to Montrovia to protect the Prince?"

"You know we're not supposed to talk about our missions."

"Are you still on a mission?"

"Yes, kind of."

"And you will continue to pretend to be this Huntley Von whatever?"

"Yes."

"*That's* why everyone is dead."

"How could that have anything to do with it?"

"Do you remember E? He was a former graduate who came back to train us on team tactics."

"Of course, I remember him. He was my—first."

"Like sexually?"

"Even though you and I were in the same class, I'd been at Blackwood since I was twelve."

"How could that be? The minimum age is eighteen."

"Josh, how did you end up at Blackwood?" I think about what Terrance suggested. That the school had been created for me. I thought it ludicrous at the time, but now I'm starting to wonder.

"I got in trouble."

"Doing what?"

"What didn't I do would be the better question, but mostly I did extreme stunts that weren't always exactly legal. Did you not research me when I told you my real name? That's the reason I told you. I thought my stunt videos would impress you. Anyway, I was doing all these videos, and the response was overwhelming, so I started doing bigger and crazier stunts. What started out as skateboarding jumps off roofs turned into base-jumping off a skyscraper. The last one, I free climbed a construction crane that was forty-four stories tall and hung off of it."

"That sounds equally amazing and stupid."

"I'm doing all this stuff without getting caught, loving the thrill and adrenaline rush. So, of course, I suggested that our senior class do an epic prank."

"What did you do?"

"Honestly, it was stupid, but it was funny. We broke into the school and stole the principal's desk, which we then managed to hoist on top of school's roof. Then we put mannequins dressed like the school principal and secretary doing it over the desk. It was hilarious. Unfortunately, not everyone thought so. I got kicked out of school right before graduation. The school pressed charges, and I was found guilty—not too tough when the video of it had gone viral. A guy came to our house before I was supposed to go to prison. He offered to have my record erased if I'd go to Blackwood. I said no. He left his card. A few days later, my family—Mom, Dad, and my little sister—were killed in an auto accident. It's said my father was driving while drunk and drove straight off a cliff. Which was odd considering my father never drank. But maybe when your only son is going to prison, you make an exception."

"You told me you were recruited because of your test scores—that they were nearly perfect."

"They were. I just omitted the other part."

"Why?"

"I had a crush on you since we first met, but you weren't interested in me until this year."

"I thought you were immature."

"I probably was. Tell me about E."

"There isn't much to tell. It was my fifteenth birthday. I was in the school's kitchen, a cupcake in hand, ready to make my wish, when he walked in looking for a snack. What happened next was sort of a blur. I blew out the candle. Then we kissed."

"And he took your virginity? That night?"

"Yeah."

"How old was he?"

"Nineteen."

"Jeeze. That's illegal."

"It didn't feel illegal, Josh."

"He took advantage of you."

I shake my head. "No, he didn't. If anything, I took advantage of him. I had a crush on him. I knew his habits. When I blew out the candle, he was my wish."

Josh wraps me in a hug like I need one. I pull away,

still gripping the gun tightly. I'm not sure what the hell is going on here. No way everyone is dead. They can't be.

"Sex is just sex, Josh. The means to an end. Isn't that what they taught us? That you can and should use sex to your advantage?"

"Yeah, but you just never seemed that way. You impressed the hell out of me with your skill at—well, everything—but there's a softness inside you that you don't let many people see."

"So back to graduation."

"I believe they are cleaning house because of you. Just what kind of a mission are you on?"

"I'm not sure."

"How many people did you interact with at Blackwood during your time here?"

"There were eight students when I arrived along with four instructors, the Dean and his secretary, two kitchen staff and two cleaning crew. Four came my second year, four more my third year, and then our class had ten, including me. Twenty-six students—all the letters of the alphabet."

"So with the staff, that means thirty-six people know the truth about you. Thirty-six people who know you're not really Ares Von Allister's long lost daughter," Josh states. "Thirty-three of which are now dead. That leaves three. Me, you, the Dean."

"How do I know you didn't kill them, Josh?" I ask, pointing the gun at him. "We were all well-trained. Why are you the only one who got away?"

"The two assailants came in from the back and opened fire. I managed to dive behind the stage steps and hide while I tried to assess my options. From what I could see, everyone was down but me. The pair was now going row by row and finishing off anyone who wasn't already dead. One of them came to check the bodies on the stage. I ambushed him, took possession of his gun, and shot the other assailant."

"And then what?"

"I took off their masks. One was E. The other was A."

"Two former students were the shooters? That makes no sense."

"It does if they work the same place you do. Who do you work for?"

"Have you ever heard of Black X?"

"No, what is it?"

"Are you sure you've never heard of it? Think. When they talked to you about what you would do after graduation, wasn't it ever mentioned?"

"No. It wasn't. Not that it matters now. You have to help me, X. In the twelve hours I've been gone, someone came in and cleaned all this up. The bodies, the carnage, it's all gone. All our possessions. Every single file. Every trace of any of us is gone. And as soon as they figure out I'm not dead, they'll come after me."

"And you've never heard of a covert organization called Black X? I'm pretty sure it's how Blackwood Academy got its name."

"Never have I ever," he says, making a little joke.

I make a quick decision and stuff the gun into my waistband. "Come with me, Josh. We need to get out of here and figure this all out."

"WHAT DID YOU do!?" the former Dean of Blackwood Academy yells, spittle flying out of his mouth, as he storms into the leader of Black X's office.

"What are you talking about, old man?"

"Graduation was supposed to be today. I went. No one was there. *Nothing* was there."

"Due to a situation, graduation was held yesterday. You must not have gotten the memo."

"Where are my students? What did you do?"

"I did what I had to."

"Tell me where they are!"

"They are dead," the leader says.

The fear of this has been sitting in his stomach since he arrived at the school to find it not only empty, but completely cleansed. He knew the school would be closing, but the current students had still been living there.

"Why? Why did you have me train them only to kill them? They could have helped us here like the other graduates have!"

"I'm afraid the other graduates along with the staff are dead as well."

"You wiped out most of our organization?" Tears fill the old man's eyes. Spies aren't supposed to get emotionally attached, but he isn't a spy anymore. He had become like a father to those young men and women. He had taken pride in their advancement.

"We can only afford to have those who we explicitly trust."

"Who does that even leave us with? A concierge, an anthropologist who likes to shop, a decrepit spy, a couple hackers, and The Ghost? How are we supposed to run an operation with so few?"

"You forgot to mention Aristotle and Huntley. The rest of them have served their purpose and had to be eliminated."

He touches a photo on the leader's desk. "She would be ashamed of what you've become."

"They killed her because of me—because of the mission I sent her on—and I will do *whatever* it takes to destroy them."

"Wouldn't it just be easier to let the Ghost kill them?"

"Their plot runs deep. Cutting off the head of the

snake will not cause it to die. It will simply rise again in another form."

"Does X know?" he asks. "Those were her friends."

"You trained those young men and women admirably. You taught them to survive on their own. She does not know the fate of her former classmates, and she must never find out."

"I quit," the Dean says.

"You owe me your life. I could have let you go to graduation and suffer the same fate."

"So it's come to this? You don't even trust me?"

"I do trust you. That's why you are still alive. And I need you to continue to monitor her. She trusts you."

"So you're only keeping me alive because I'm useful?"

"Yes, and you would be wise to remember that fact."

THE OLD MAN flips him off as he exits the room. He knows he deserves it but he can't be swayed by the old man's emotion. He slides his hand down the photo, remembering how she called him right before she died. How she told him she had figured it out. How they would meet the next morning.

His thoughts are interrupted by a computer beep, indicating a secure email from one of his sources in the Middle East.

He reads it, then picks up his phone, hits a button, and says, "We need to talk."

A few minutes later, the Ghost enters his office. "I was on my way in here when you called. We have a big problem. One of the graduates managed to escape."

"How did that happen?"

"He was well-trained, I assume. But it gets worse. He took the men's hoods off and knows two former graduates were sent to kill them. I've cleaned up the mess, disposed of the bodies, and the school has been cleansed. No one will ever know what happened, unless—"

"He talks," the man says. "Do you know where he is?"

"No idea. I'd ask the old man for help, but he's not going to be happy to learn that we disposed of his former students and staff."

"He already knows, but don't worry, I'll deal with him. We did what we had to do. I would have preferred to use them in our fight. They were well-trained. But with X's high profile, it was inevitable that someone would make contact with her. We couldn't risk blowing her cover."

The Ghost nods in agreement. He understands sometimes there is collateral damage on the path to justice. "If you would have let me take care of it as I requested, it would be done. Now we have dangerous threads blowing in the wind. One little pull could unravel what's left of our organization."

"Something curious has happened in the world today," the leader says, indicating their previous conversation is over. "We know part of their plan hinged on controlling the Strait of Montrovia. I just received a tip from a source that the Syrian government has seized control of the Russian port in Tartus."

"Are they crazy? Russia will destroy them."

"It's my understanding that Russia is trying to work on a *diplomatic* solution, which will take too long. We have to do something."

"Why was this not on the news?" the Ghost wonders.

"Because it's not as sensational as the President's funeral."

"And you believe this is related to Montrovia? I don't understand why they would want Tartus? It seems so random."

The leader points to a map on the wall. "The Strait of Montrovia controls access from the Mediterranean Sea to the Atlantic Ocean. Without access to an ocean, you don't have access to the world. European countries rely on the sea to export goods. Russia is rearming. They have made huge increases to their military budget, including a jump of nearly $11 billion over the last year. But all that will do them no good if their ships can't get anywhere. Tartus is their *only* deep, warm water port. From Tartus, Russia can project its naval power anywhere in the world. All of its other ports are either ice-locked for some of the year or landlocked, which requires them to pass through straits controlled by other countries. My guess is that they are trying to cripple the world's military superpowers, so when the time comes, they will be ham-stringed in the fight."

"The old saying goes that if you control the oil, you control the world."

"It also goes on to say that if you control the food, you control the people," the leader adds. "Maybe that's a future step, but before you can control the people, you have to be able to their cripple governments, simultaneously. And what better time to do it than when the world is preoccupied with the death of a President?"

"We need to figure out their plan. I fear we don't have much time."

The leader leans way back in his chair, thinking.

The Ghost takes a seat, keeping his thoughts to himself. He knows better than to interrupt the leader's process, simply watching him as he leans forward, places his elbows on the desk, and steeples his fingers, pressing them against his lower lip.

After a couple of long minutes, the leader speaks. "I have a plan to kill multiple birds with the same stone."

"How so?" the Ghost asks.

"Think about it. No one knows where the student has been while he was at Blackwood. We create travel documents proving he's been in Syria and pin the assassination of the President on him. There will be a world-wide manhunt. Once they arrest him, we'll know where he is, and you can take him out. Problem solved. In the meanwhile, our new President needs to make a bold statement to the world. Our government will retaliate against the terror organizations in Syria for the President's death, and in doing so, will take control of both the country and the Russian port. We rid ourselves of our problem and foil their plan all at the same time."

The Ghost leans back in his chair and smiles. "That's brilliant."

"Make it happen," he says.

TOGETHER, JOSH AND I carefully exit the mansion, move slowly past the out buildings, and make our way to my car.

Josh whistles. "Nice ride."

"Perk of my cover," I say, starting the car. There's a good song on the radio, so I turn it up and take off, not really sure where to go, but needing to think.

The music is interrupted by an announcement. "Breaking news. The FBI has begun a nationwide manhunt in conjunction with the assassination of the President. The fugitive's name is Josh Bentley. He's a five-foot eleven inch, one hundred and seventy pound, twenty-one-year-old Caucasian with dark hair and brown eyes. If you see a man of this description, do not attempt to detain him. Call the authorities immediately."

"Josh! They're saying *you* killed the President! Why would they say that?"

"They know that I'm not dead—that I escaped. They're manipulating the press to try to find me."

"You think Black X has the power to manipulate the entire country?"

"But it makes sense that I shot the President of the freaking United States? The country I have trained to serve?"

"No. Merda. This is a mess."

"What am I going to do? If they find me, they'll kill me."

"I think I know where we need to go," I say, a plan coming together in my head.

I check my speed. The last thing we need right now is to get pulled over.

I hold my hand up, thinking, running through all I know and wondering if I'm correct in believing Josh as I drive toward the one man who might be able to help him. Once I'm on the highway and headed to my destination, I put the SIM card back in my phone and turn it on. I don't know if I'm being tracked, but it's probably best not to appear off grid right now.

WHEN WE ARRIVE at the upscale mall, Josh looks at me like I'm nuts. "I know you're driving a Ferrari and have loads of money, but maybe now is not the best time for shopping?"

I park near the store's back exit, grab the business card, run my hands through Josh's hair so it sticks up artfully, and say, "Just follow my lead."

"You're not turning me in, are you?"

"I hope not."

"Well, that's reassuring."

We go into the boutique, where we are immediately greeted. I flash the card. "I have an appointment with Mr. Gallagher at four."

The sales clerk studies us with a calculating glare, and I'm praying she hasn't seen the news.

"Follow me," she finally says, then proceeds to lead us to a dressing room, which she unlocks. "Wait in here." She shuts the door, inserts the key, and locks us in the room.

"She knows," he says, looking panicked. "She's locked us in and is going to call the cops."

"Shh. Stop worrying. You know we could pick that lock in a heartbeat."

"Do you still have my gun? Are you armed?" He smiles. The first time since he found me at school. "Not that you need to be."

We turn when we hear a scraping noise and see the trendy reclaimed wood wall behind us slide open.

"Is this your secret headquarters?" he asks, his eyes

getting huge. "How cool."

The parting of the wall reveals an elevator. We step inside, noticing there are no numbers for us to push. When the doors reopen, Intrepid is waiting.

"You were supposed to come alone," he chastises.

"I'm going to dinner at the Montrovian Embassy tonight and need a cute clutch to match my gown."

Gallagher lets out a chuckle, shakes his head at me, and leads us to an office. "So who is your friend?"

"Have you seen the news? Apparently, he killed the President."

Gallagher's eyes bulge. "What?"

"Turn on the television."

He clicks a remote and is immediately rewarded with a photo of Josh. The announcer reports that Josh was sentenced to prison a few years ago but never showed up for his term. That there is an outstanding warrant for his arrest, and he is to be considered armed and dangerous. Then some theory that he made his way to Syria where he was trained by a terror group and sent back to kill the President.

Gallagher twirls a pen in his hand and watches the television with amusement. "That's all pretty convenient, isn't it? The evidence all laid out? So how do you know him, and why did you bring him here?"

"Do you remember when I told you I work for Black X?"

"Yes, that's what I wanted to talk to you about today. I hadn't heard that name in years."

"What do you know about it?"

"I believe the case had something to do with the Georgia Guidestones—have you heard of them?"

Josh and I shake our heads.

"How it was erected and who paid for it is a mystery, but the large monument appeared in 1980, is reminiscent of Stonehenge, and is said to be a guide for our future world. The most widely agreed-upon interpretation is that the Stones describe how to rebuild the world after some kind of massive, devastating population reduction, possibly nuclear war. Conspiracy theorists believe it was put up by a group whose goal it is to create this new world."

"How will they do that?" Josh asks, enthralled.

"That's where we get into the conspiracy theories. Mostly revolving around the first guide, which is to maintain humanity under five hundred million. Considering the world population is currently at somewhere around seven billion, that would mean a ninety-three percent reduction. Conspiracy theorists say we are being poisoned by fluoride in our water, chemtrails, genetically modified grains, soft drinks, fast food. You name it, there's a conspiracy theory about it. But most of them lead to something called 'The Great Culling,' which is believed to be—now this is where it gets a little crazy—something planned by either Satan, the Illuminati, the Masons, the very wealthy, or aliens—depending on the theory—as a way to wean out the weak gene pool and to allow only the strong, or possibly the very rich, to survive. Black X was the name of a study that was trying to discover if there was any truth to the theories. I couldn't remember much more or what the outcome was, so I looked it up in our database."

"What did you find out?"

"Nothing. Not one single thing. Which in and of itself is very odd. We British pride ourselves on our due diligence. If I heard it in the office, someone would have documented it."

"Are you saying it was purposefully deleted or classified higher than your pay grade?"

"I have the highest security clearance there is. And because I am curious by nature, I had our men hack into the database at Langley. Also, came up empty. How did you come to work for Black X?"

"Are you going to document what I tell you in your database?"

"No. Our conversation is off the record."

"I find that hard to believe," Josh interrupts. "More than likely everything we've said so far has been recorded. Don't tell him, X. We shouldn't trust him."

"Did he just call you *X*?"

I nod. "Are you recording us?"

"No. You have my word."

"I don't trust him," Josh says.

I level my gaze at Intrepid then turn to Josh. "You have no choice but to trust him. Because I already do."

I know I should hold back and tell him only what he needs to know, but I don't. I give him the condensed version of everything from my mother's death forward, ending with the massacre at our school, what I overheard the Director of the CIA say, and the conspiracy theories on my mother's locket.

He listens intently, clearly absorbing it all and combining his knowledge to come to a conclusion. I expect him to have something profound to say, some way to figure this all out.

Instead, he says, "Was your mother Charlotte Cassleberry?"

"Yes, did you know her?"

"I did not know her personally, but I do remember hearing about an American agent being assassinated and how they never found her daughter. It was heartbreaking to those of us in the business." He studies the ceiling. "The CIA couldn't find you and presumed you were dead. They didn't want to admit two of their best agents were killed on their home turf, so they covered it up by saying you all died in an automobile accident."

"I think so."

"So let me get this straight—a man who was a friend

of your father sent you to this school and trained you—"

"He didn't train me. He just sent me there. I only saw him a few times."

He keeps going. He's on a roll now. "Your call sign was *X*, and you now work for *Black X*, who just killed off all the students at your school, so as not to blow *your* cover and when they realized Josh, here, was still alive they *framed him* for the murder of the President?"

"Sounds crazy, but yes, that's correct."

"What is your current mission?"

"I was told a mission was forthcoming, but I'll be going after the man who assassinated the President."

"How will you be notified?"

"I'm not sure. Protecting Lorenzo was my very first mission, and I received that in writing at my school."

My phone buzzes, causing me to glance down. An unknown number has sent me a text containing only a link. I double check that my secure network is enabled and click on it.

A blank page with no apparent web address appears. When I scroll down the page, there is a message.

Your mission, should you choose to *accept it:* Track down the assassin who killed the President of the United States, *uncover* who paid for the hit, and *eliminate* the assassin.

When I hold it up for Intrepid to read, the message

disappears.

"What did it say?" he asks.

"They want me to find out who paid for the hit on the President and eliminate the assassin. Does that mean they want me to find Josh and kill him?"

"That's awkward," Josh deadpans.

"I need to get in touch with them."

I call my emergency protocol number, and after a series of clicks, someone answers. The voice is distorted, so I have no idea if it's a man or woman.

"Your authentication code?"

I recite it.

"What do you need?"

"I received a mission and need clarification."

"Please hold."

I put the phone on speaker so Josh and Intrepid can hear.

A slightly different mechanical voice fills the room. "X, your mission is clear."

"So, I'm supposed to kill Josh?"

"That was a bit of misdirection. Don't worry about Josh. We have him safely hidden away. We want to give you time to get to the assassin without interference from other agencies."

"So other agencies don't know who the real assassin is?"

"Not yet."

"It feels like there is something you aren't telling me. What aren't you saying?"

"I'm saying it's in your best interest to follow orders."

"Yes, but I can't do my job if I don't have the necessary background information."

"In this business, it's always wise to watch your back. As I taught you, the business is built on lies." No shit. He's already lied to me twice during our very short conversation.

"You taught me? Is this the Dean?"

"Yes."

"What if I want to stop being Huntley? What if I refuse this mission?"

"I'm afraid that role is now your destiny." Meaning if I don't keep being Huntley, they'll kill me too?

"Did Black X kill Ares Von Allister so we could become his heirs?"

"No."

"Can I trust you?"

"What did I teach you?"

"To never trust anyone."

"And with that I will end our call."

"Wait. The assassin who killed the President, does he have a name?"

"The Priest."

"You made me study him."

"With good reason."

"Because he killed my mother?"

"Yes," he says. The phone beeps indicating that he ended our call.

"Obviously, I'm being lied to," I state. "What if I'm working for the bad guys?"

"I don't think you are," he says. "Our agency intercepted a call. The call that sent me to Montrovia in the first place."

"What did it say?" Josh asks.

"*It starts in Montrovia.*"

"What starts?" I ask.

"That's what I was tasked to find out. Whoever you work for could very well be trying to stop a threat that is much bigger than the Prince of a small country."

"So should I go after the assassin?"

"Of course you should. That's what you wanted, right? To exact revenge."

"Yes, but I didn't expect it to be my second mission. What if I can't do it? He's supposed to be the best."

"Will your brother receive the same mission?"

"I don't know. In Montrovia, I was told to eliminate the people responsible for the threat. He was not. I'm their assassin, not Ari."

"Do you want me to come with you?" both Josh and Intrepid ask at the same time.

I shake my head. "No. I studied The Priest. He works alone. And I probably need to face him alone." I turn to Intrepid. "Can you keep Josh safe?"

"Absolutely." He stands and says to Josh, "You look like you could use food, a shower, and some shut eye."

HE ESCORTS JOSH out of the room then comes back and sits down across the table from me.

"Is Josh as well-trained as you are?"

"Josh is a daredevil, seemingly not afraid of anything. But today at school, he was very afraid—which is understandable—but I overtook him easily. At school, he was more of a challenge. He also told me his real name, something we weren't ever supposed to do. I think he could be a good agent, but I'm not sure I'd want him out in the field with me yet. What will you do with him?"

"Until the manhunt is over, we'll keep him hidden away and safe. After that, I was thinking about offering him a job. He'd start at the bottom, like we all do. I suspect he has a lot of potential."

"I can't believe they killed everyone. I feel so guilty."

"Whoever Black X is, they have gone all in on you and your brother. That's quite the gamble." He studies me. "Although after seeing what you are capable of, I understand why. What I don't understand is the high profile."

"Me either."

"And why would someone hire an assassin to kill the President? Less than five minutes after he died there was another President to take his place. Unless—"

"Unless what?"

"Your new President was in on it."

Daniel's father is a bad guy? No way.

But then I wonder.

"Daniel introduced me to Lorenzo, but he also tried to keep me away from him. He showed up at my villa at random times and showed up on the yacht without an invite."

Intrepid tilts his head, thinking. "Let me make some inquiries and get back to you."

"Okay," I say. "Do you think Lorenzo is still in danger?"

"I would say absolutely."

"Do you know any talented men who would be interested in being one of the King of Montrovia's bodyguards?"

"I might, actually."

"Get in touch with Juan. He's going to start looking for a new team." I check the clock on my phone. "Crap. I gotta go. I have an Embassy dinner tonight."

"The wheels of the political machine keep spinning even on the day of the President's funeral, huh?"

I shrug. "Apparently."

"I'll walk you out. We need to pick you out a bag on the way, otherwise your trip here may seem suspicious."

We exit from the dressing room, and Gallagher takes

me through the store, chooses two evening bags from the store's extensive collection, pays for them himself, and then walks me to my car.

"Seriously, Huntley, if you need anything, let me know."

"I brought you Josh."

"Does that mean you trust me?"

"Spies aren't supposed to trust each other," I state.

"True. But you're different from most spies I know."

I roll my eyes at him and get in the car. I start it and then roll down the window. "You're right, I am."

I GET HOME, quickly freshen up, and meet Lorenzo down in the study.

He's wearing a trim-fit suit and his hair is slicked back.

"You look beautiful," he says, taking in my red A-line cocktail dress with almost regal looking gold metallic embellishments.

"Thank you. You look beautiful yourself."

He puts his head down and blushes slightly. It's adorable.

"I have a gift for you."

"What for?"

"To celebrate your knighthood." He hands me a white box tied with a lush, black velvet ribbon.

I open it.

"Is this a crown?"

"Actually, it's a coronet."

"It looks like a crown."

"It's not a crown. A crown is what I wore at my coronation. Crowns have high arches and are worn only by royalty. A coronet symbolizes nobility."

"What about tiaras?"

"Tiaras are a type of crown, as is a coronet, but a tiara has a semi-circular base as opposed to a full one. And there are different styles of tiaras for different occasions. When we are back in Montrovia, we can revisit the Royal Vault where I will show you the intricate variations. But for now—may I?"

I nod, so he places it on my head, then stands back and takes me in. "Perfection."

"You shouldn't have bought me this."

"Oh, I didn't," he says with a grin. "It's a tradition. The country gives them out to its newest nobility."

"You forget I am trained in deception indicators. You paused your speech and touched your eyebrow. You're lying to me."

He gives me a smirk. "Fine. It is a gift from me, Contessa." He holds out his elbow. "Shall we go?"

THE MONTROVIAN EMBASSY is gorgeous and screams old world wealth. After cocktails and introductions in the main floor salon, we are taken to the fifth floor ballroom for dinner. The room features what must be centuries-old chandeliers, lush gold velvet draperies, and a domed, stained glass ceiling.

Lorenzo and I are seated in a place of honor with the Montrovian Ambassador and the Danish Prince. There is just one long table set up in the middle of the room as there are only about thirty in attendance, one of whom is not Aleksandr Nikolaevich. *Guess the CIA doesn't know everything.*

AFTER A WONDERFUL five-course dinner, a dessert station is rolled into the room, featuring handmade crepes with numerous fillings.

"What is your preference, my dear?" Lorenzo asks me. "Sweet or savory?"

I look into his eyes dreamily. "Say that again."

"Sweet—?

"No say, *savory.*" He says it again, his accent sounding particularly delicious. "That sounds so sexy. I must have that kind."

He gazes into my eyes, and we share a moment. The kind of moment from a love story—two people rooted in their spots, the world spinning around them, while they see only each other. They say we only use a small portion of our brain. That we could speak telepathically if we used our full capacity. It's moments like this where I feel like I already can. It's different than an intuitive feeling—deeper. A delicate mix of body, brain, and hormones that causes a strong feeling somewhere deep inside me.

Making me feel like I've met *the one*.

I vowed if I ever met the one I would run in the other direction, but instead I find myself inexplicably pulled to do the opposite—run straight to him and never leave.

Except I have to leave.

Soon.

THE ATTENDEES BID us farewell after enjoying coffee and conversation. Lorenzo takes me back up to the ballroom and asks for a dance.

When I'm held tightly in his arms, it's really hard not to be swept away.

"As much as I'm enjoying my evening with you, Lorenzo, I know stolen kisses and these wonderful shared moments aren't going to keep you happy."

"My mother asked of you," he replies, changing the subject. "She likes you. Both my parents like you." He stops and shakes his head. "I forget that he's gone sometimes. Does the grief ever get better?"

"You never get over it. You just have to move on, for them. Your father was proud of you, and any criticism he gave you was only his attempt to make you a better future King. He had already raised a good man."

"Other women I have dated would not be so kind. I believed I would never be happy with just one woman, not when there are so many beautiful distractions in the world." He cups my cheek in his hand. "Until you."

"Lorenzo."

"Huntley, I don't care how you make your living. I want to continue to court you." He takes my hand and pulls me close. "And even though I know with certainty that you could probably kill me in a few seconds if you wanted, I like the danger. Just think, when we marry, I could fire Juan. You could be both my princess and my bodyguard."

I laugh nervously, trying to lighten the mood. "You're silly. I'm not even sure when I'll see you again. I received a new mission today."

"Does it have to do with the President's death?"

"Yes, I'll be going after the assassin."

"Would it make a difference if I said I wish you wouldn't go?"

"This is why people like me can't have emotional entanglements."

He is not deterred. "Well, like it or not, now you have someone to come home to." He looks distraught but quickly changes the subject. "My parents had an arranged marriage."

"They did? That surprises me. They seemed in love."

"While they were not in love when they married,

they did grow to love each other. An arranged marriage will be my fate, unless—"

His words hang there.

"Lorenzo, not only did this person kill the President, but he killed my mother."

"So once you succeed, you will have your revenge?"

"He's the best assassin in the world."

"You could turn down the mission."

"You know why I can't do that. You also need to know there's a very real possibility that I won't succeed. That I won't be back."

"You have to come back, Lee," he says, cradling my face in his hands. "Because I think I love you."

Tears threaten as I feel a crack in my shell. I think that's what happens when you experience loss. You wrap a protective shell around yourself, so no one else can ever get in. So you'll never feel the pain of losing a loved one again. I've carefully built up my walls and put my emotions aside to train for this day, and now that it's here—now that I'm going to do it, instead of feeling like the lethal weapon that I am—I feel torn. This moment is everything I've worked for.

"Do you return my affection, Lee?"

I shake my head, knowing my eyes betray me.

A text interrupts our moment.

We have located him. A car is waiting for you outside the Embassy. You must go immediately.

Time is of the essence.

I lean toward Lorenzo, giving him a quick peck goodbye. He wraps his arms around me and deepens the kiss, his tongue like an elixir, causing visions of a life of love and happiness.

A life that cannot be my destiny.

"I have to go," I say quietly then walk away.

It takes every ounce of strength I have not to turn around and look at him one last time. Instead, I race down the stairs and out to the car, where Ari is waiting.

"Where are we going?"

"To the airport."

I don't say anything else until we are dropped off on the tarmac of an Air Force base. "What are we doing here?"

"You don't get motion sickness, do you?"

"Uh, no. Why?"

He points to two F-16B fighter jets sitting in ready. "Those are our rides."

My eyes get huge. "What?! Where are we going?"

"France. Quickly."

"WELL, I'LL BE. Now this ain't something you see every day," a handsome pilot says, after giving me a once over and scrutinizing my ornate dress and high heels. "I'm Lieutenant Captain Collin Morgan, call sign Cobra, and this is my wingman Lieutenant Captain, Mark Arnold, call sign Razor."

"How'd you two manage this?" Razor asks. "Friends in high places?"

"We're trying to avoid customs," Ari jokes.

Razor turns up his nose at us, but Cobra flirts with me. "You're about to get the ride of your life, princess." It's then that I realize I'm still wearing the coronet. "Going to a party?"

"Well, you know, it's hard to be popular," I joke.

"You look familiar—wait, you're the chick who was at the President's swearing in, aren't you?"

"Guilty."

"It makes sense now. Are you really going to a party?"

"Kind of." I nod, figuring I might as well keep up the charade.

"And we don't have much time," Ari stresses as he watches precious seconds tick away on his watch. "I assume you were told of our tight schedule?"

"Of course. We have two fighters fueled and ready. There are flight suits for you in here." He leads us into a locker room. "Get them on and meet us on the tarmac. When the Commander-in-Chief wants something done, you do it."

If the President did approve this—which I highly doubt, I don't think they would have mentioned the assassin they were sending was the same girl who slept with his son. Not that it really matters. I haven't heard from his son since he told me I couldn't go to the funeral with him.

Ari slides his flight suit on over his clothes and is quickly out the door.

I try to stuff the full skirt of my dress into the suit, but it won't fit.

With no time left, I strip it off, throw on the flight suit, grab my heels and handbag, and then run back outside.

I GET BUCKLED in, am taught how to put the oxygen mask on my helmet, how to eject out of the plane if necessary, and am given a barf bag along with a smirk.

"I'm not using this," I say, handing it back to the pilot. There's no freaking way I will allow myself to puke.

In a few moments, we are hurtling down the runway, and I can feel the weight of the g-forces as the fighter ascends into the night sky.

We climb high quickly, and I am able to listen in on the pilots' chatter.

Once we are at Mach Two, Ari asks if I can hear him.

"I hear you," I reply.

"Are you doing okay?" he asks. "Do you feel sick?"

"I'm fine," I reply, even though I am a little queasy.

"This is crazy."

"You should take a nap if you can," Ari suggests. "We have to hit the ground running."

The pilots say very little during the flight. I'm not sure if it's normal or if they were told not to ask or tell.

The fighter veers and changes direction causing my stomach to flip again. The amazing savory crepes trying to come back up make me think of Lorenzo, of what he said tonight.

Avionic controls flicker with activity in front of me. I focus on them, trying to clear my mind. Although I've never flown a plane, I was taught to in flight simulators, so if it was necessary, I could get by.

That was one of my goals after graduation—to get behind the controls of a real plane. Although this isn't exactly how I pictured it—in a fighter jet being raced toward Paris and my mother's assassin.

I can see stars through the canopy as well as the other fighter just off the starboard wing. I close my eyes and try to rest, but I can't.

Instead, I visualize my mission. How each disguise will work. Step by step how I will track the assassin.

And, of course, exactly how I plan to kill him.

MISSION: DAY FIVE

WE LAND AT a French air base less than ten miles from Paris, get out of the plane quickly, and are rushed by the pilots into a locker room.

"You survived," the hotshot Cobra says to me.

"No thanks to you. Somehow I don't think all those turn and burns were necessary. Were you trying to make me sick?"

"Yes, ma'am," he says in an adorable southern accent, making it hard to be mad at him. He reaches for my front zipper. "Don't forget to leave my flight suit."

I back up. "Um, I can't take it off right now."

"Why not?"

"Because the dress I was wearing when I arrived wouldn't exactly fit under it."

He cocks his head and smirks. "Are you tellin' me

that you're nekked under there?"

"Almost," I reply.

"Well, hell, darling. I hate to tell you this, but that there suit is the property of the United States government. I can't allow you to leave here with it."

"Fine," I reply, stripping out of it, and now wearing nothing but my strapless bra and black lace thong.

"It's like I'm livin' a fantasy."

Ari walks by. "What the heck?"

"The pilot needs his flight suit back. Said I couldn't leave. And we need to leave now. I'll find clothes later."

Ari rushes off and comes back with a towel, wrapping it around me.

"You're being weird."

"I don't need to see my sister like that," he says, rushing me out to our car.

"Thanks for the ride, guys," I say, waving goodbye with my evening bag.

"The backpack you requested is supposed to be waiting in the car," Ari says as we get in.

"And hopefully some weapons," I add.

THANKFULLY, WE HAVE both in the car, and the backpack is set up exactly the way I asked. I quickly throw on my first outfit, which is a goth/biker chick look, and apply makeup while Ari drives.

GPS says we will arrive at the location where the hit

is supposed to take place in twenty minutes—putting us there in just under four hours.

Once I am dressed and made up, I go through the other items in the car.

"What all did they give us?" Ari asks.

"There's a backpack for you with a change of clothes and an iPad. Two handguns—Glock for you. Sig Sauer for me. Keys to a motorbike that's parked just around corner from the hit location. A remote controlled, palm-sized drone for additional surveillance. Button-shaped pins that allow Terrance to see and hear us. And earpieces so we can hear him."

"How do you feel about that?" Ari asks.

"What do you mean?"

"Do you think having Terrance in our ear will be a help or a hindrance?"

"I think talking into our cuff will look pretty suspicious to an assassin."

"We can't risk spooking him."

I can't help but laugh.

"What's so funny?"

"You said we can't spook him. That's funny since we are spooks."

"I don't get it."

"Haven't you ever heard a spy called a spook?"

"Uh, no. Why are they called that?"

"Because they are supposed to be invisible. Like a

ghost. Get it?"

"Spooks, huh?" he says, nodding his head, like he finally gets it.

"Whatever. Anyway, that's why having Terrance in our ear will be invaluable. He can hack into traffic cameras to keep an eye on the assassin, making us virtually undetectable." I hand him a small, clear earpiece. "Here, put this in and let's make sure it all works."

"I'm more concerned about my gun working," he says. "How does it look?"

"Freshly cleaned and oiled. Extra magazines."

While Ari continues to race toward our destination, I get the button positioned properly on each of us, put my earpiece in, and make contact with Terrance.

"Can you hear us, T?" I ask.

"Do I have a code name now, Spy Girl?"

I laugh. "Apparently. I take it you can hear us. Are you getting visuals, as well?"

"Yes, we're up and running. Are you going to make it in time?"

"We are," Ari replies, glancing at the clock, gripping the wheel, and pressing down a little harder on the gas pedal. Then he goes, "Spy Girl?"

Terrance laughs in our ears.

WE ARRIVE AT the given address and discover it's the

location of a coffee shop. Ari drives past it and parks as I take in the neighborhood. It's morning in France, but most people are already at work, and traffic is minimal.

"What's the plan?" Ari asks. "Should we go inside or sit on the patio?"

"He shot the President with a sniper rifle. I feel like one of us should be on higher ground."

"Should we send up the drone for that?"

"Maybe. I just wish we knew how he was going to kill his target."

"What would you do?" he asks, which helps me visualize the process.

"It would depend what I was told about the target. For example, if the target goes to the coffee shop every day and sits inside to read the morning paper, I could poison the coffee, shoot the target with a poison dart, follow him into the bathroom and drown him, or just slit his throat. But any of those ways would mean he would die while I was there, and I wouldn't want that. Since the place isn't crowded, I'd want it to look like a heart attack or that the target had fallen asleep. It would take a waiter a bit to realize it, and I'd have already paid for my coffee and walked out the door. I could even walk by the target on my way out, bump into him, and administer a slow poison into his arm. I'd be gone before he died, and no one would be the wiser. What would you do, Ari?"

"I guess I missed class the day we had assassin training. I'd put on a mask, walk in, shoot him in the head, and walk out."

"No messing around with you. You're all force and no subtlety." I give him a smile. "I will say though, you've been doing a fine job of playing my brother."

"What's with the look?" he asks, eyeing my first disguise. "You certainly don't look like Huntley."

"That's the point." I put my chin down and speak to the button. "The drone is in my palm. She's all yours now, Terrance." There's no reply, but the little drone starts with a small buzzing sound then lifts off into the sky. "Why don't you take up a position at the bus stop, Ari. Maybe buy a paper and sit on the bench. I'll position the motorbike just down the street." I check my watch. "We have two minutes. Let's split up."

Ari buys a newspaper and takes his position on the bench. I'm on the motorbike, having just come around the corner, when I hear him shouting.

"Oh my God! The target is Clarice Vallenta. I repeat . . . the target is Clarice!"

"We have to stop it," I yell back. "Go!"

The sound of a gun's retort cracks through the air, and I watch as Clarice goes down in the middle of the street.

"Help her and try to search her house for clues, Ari. I'll go after the assassin."

ARI DROPS HIS newspaper and rushes into the street. Clarice has been mortally wounded and is quickly bleeding out.

"Your sister was killed because of her plan for Montrovia. Don't let them get away with killing you, too. What do you know?"

"Money," Clarice whispers. "Ophelia money."

He knows police procedure says he shouldn't move her, but he does anyway, pulling her out of the street and into the doorway she came out of.

Ari knows Clarice is dying, but he takes his jacket off and holds it against the wounds on her chest, trying to stop the bleeding. There's nothing he can do. He's studied what happens when you get shot in the chest. From front to back, the bullet obliterates all the tissue near it. Even if the heart weren't struck directly, it would have ruptured, leading to catastrophic hemorrhaging. In military school, he watched videos of men dying in battle and although tragic, it's honorable. This is not an honorable death.

He cradles her head in his lap. "It will be okay," he lies, as her reflexive breathing efforts continue. She's not only bleeding from her wounds but also from her nose and mouth. She coughs, gurgles, and tries to get oxygen from her pierced lungs.

Her breathing slows, and her eyes become fixed upon him as her fight is over.

He checks her pulse, confirms her death, and closes her eyes. Then he slides gloves over his hands and does a quick search of her house, looking for any possible clues.

"Watch for the police," Ari says out loud, knowing Terrance can hear him. "And tell me if you see anything I miss."

In the first bedroom, which he assumes is Clarice's based on the pink and purple paisley wallpaper, lace bedspread, and hippie looking clothing tossed about, he finds a notebook with a ribbon tied around it full of clippings. He doesn't have time to go through it, just stuffs it in his backpack. He finds a laptop on the desk, turns it on, inserts a flash drive, and copies its contents, hoping any monetary transactions would be in its files. Could her sister have been paid to take over Montrovia? Had someone already given her payment for the Strait and wants it back?

He leaves Clarice's room and searches the kitchen, finding a stack of cash in the freezer and taking it. Maybe this is the money she was referring to. They can trace the cash and have it analyzed for fingerprints. Finding nothing else of interest, he moves to the living room. The model of the envisioned Montrovia is not there, just a photo of Clarice and Ophelia, the two girls arm in arm.

He goes across the hall and finds a closed door. Cautiously opening it, he discovers Ophelia's room.

It is the complete opposite of her sister's.

Pale grey walls, pristine white bedding. Everything neat and orderly.

There are a few photos of her and Viktor together. Viktor has money, he thinks.

He checks his watch. He's been searching the house for two minutes. Although he managed to get Clarice out of the street quickly, someone will have called the police.

He needs to call them too.

He takes out his phone, makes a frantic call, and knows he doesn't have much time left.

He wonders why Black X didn't have them continue their mission. Why didn't they investigate Ophelia and Clarice? Was there more to it? Did they believe killing Lorenzo was simply fueled by her hatred for her father? That's it, her father, his death started it all. Who killed him and why? Or did they believe it stopped with her? Is Lorenzo still in danger? If there is a bigger plot, he most definitely could be.

He looks under the bed, under the mattress, and through the organized bookshelves. No books on money, mostly French history, poetry, and art. Notably not a single book about anything Montrovian.

The sounds of sirens are getting closer. He checks the bookcase and the desk for hidden panels, and then moves to the closet. It is almost completely bare, not even a stray hanger. All that is there is a shoebox sitting on a shelf. He flips the lid, hoping to find something, but instead he finds it empty.

Which is odd. Why would it be here?

Afraid it could be important, he shoves it in his backpack, then returns to the computer and pulls out the flash drive.

He runs back to the entry where Clarice's body still lies—blood pooling under her. He digs in her jacket for her phone, finding it and scrolling through the recent call list.

"Are you getting all this?" he asks Terrance, holding the phone up so the camera can record this for later.

Then he sees that she has messages from her boy-friend, urging her to see him. Sixteen of them actually, since the death of her sister.

"Bring the phone with you," Terrance instructs. "The police are close."

Ari rushes out of the home, noting the siren does sound much closer. He quickly throws his backpack in the car and then rushes back to the dead body.

"You can't be calm when the police arrive," Terrance yells in his ear, but he knows this and is already mentally working himself up.

When the police arrive, they are greeted with the sorrowful scene of a handsome man cradling a beautiful girl's lifeless body, smoothing her hair, and telling her repeatedly that help is coming and to just hang on.

The man is obviously in shock.

And the girl is quite dead.

They question the man, and upon discovering that the woman is former royalty and a friend of his, they take down Ari Von Allister's passport number, pat him on the back in condolence, drive him to a hotel, and request he stay in town overnight.

I SEE THE muzzle flash from the corner of my eye and quickly determine which building it came from—four stories over a restaurant.

But if the assassin is as good as they say, I know he will simply walk out the front door. The restaurant will remember a business man with a briefcase who had brunch, tipped well, but spent a few moments longer than he should have in the public loo, probably indigestion from his busy life. Or he could have been carrying a shopping bag, pretending to be a tourist. He'd have a map and a guidebook of walking tours through Paris. He'd tell the story of how he got off the trail and stumbled upon the quaint restaurant, which is clearly a hidden gem.

In a perfect operation, I would send Ari to the back, just as a precaution, but I'm on my own now. Therefore, I'll have to go with my gut.

I'm going through the motions of putting my helmet on and sliding my leg around the motorbike when I spot him.

Businessman, shiny briefcase a bit larger than normal—possibly a sniper's case. The man stops and looks down the street. Seeing Ari pull a bleeding Clarice out of the street doesn't give him pause.

And I know for sure I have my man. Anyone else would be startled by the scene. He's not, because it's exactly what he expected to see.

I look downward as I start the bike, knowing the noise will cause the assassin to glance in my direction. Once it's running, I pull my phone out, pretending to call someone, as the assassin stops a taxi and gets in.

I recite the license plate for Terrance, in case my looking down caused him to miss it.

Then I take off in the opposite direction of the taxi. It's important the assassin doesn't think he's being followed.

"Don't you lose that cab, Terrance," I say.

"Don't worry. I've got it."

Above the cab is the surveillance drone, one that probably has the Von Allister stamp on it. The drone is virtually soundless, and if the assassin did happen to look up, he'd think it was a bird. It was smart we sent the drone up earlier.

"Turn left now," Terrance says. "You'll be on the street parallel to the taxi. It looks like he's headed for the train station." He gives me further directions then I park the bike and go into the station.

"Where is he?" I ask.

"I can't take the drone inside, so we're having to rely on the station's security cameras. Give us a minute."

"We don't have a minute," I say as I purchase a ticket then move to the center of the station where I spot the assassin among a group of people staring up at the arrival boards.

"I've got him," I say softly. "I'm going silent."

The assassin, along with others who are all carrying suitcases, make their way to the airport express train.

Following an assassin by myself is going to be tricky, even with a backpack full of disguises.

Right now, I'm goth girl—tatted sleeves that are really just flesh-colored hosiery with tattoos printed on them, but which look like the real thing. I have numerous fake piercings. My contact-lens-green eyes are heavily made up, but the eyeliner and heavy shadow is a sticker, expertly placed but easily removed. I choose the seat directly across from the assassin and slip my tongue out, revealing a fake piercing that is painfully clamped into place.

My gesture has the desired effect. The assassin gives me a smirk.

Truth, the assassin is quite handsome. Dark hair, stubble on his cheeks, and the kind of olive skin that both tans beautifully and makes it difficult to determine his ethnicity, but his eyes are dark and calculating in a way that defies the easy-going smirk.

Although his face is far different than I remember—most likely the work of a skilled plastic surgeon—his eyes are the same, even though he's attempting to hide them behind glasses with a heavy frame.

I could take him out right now. All I'd have to do is slip my hand inside the backpack and pull out the gun.

Bang.

My retribution would be complete.

But it wouldn't be very satisfying.

And I wouldn't properly complete my mission. I need to get him somewhere alone so that I can question him before I kill him.

I take earbuds out of my backpack and put them in, cuing up a playlist of death metal and playing it so loudly I'm sure that he can hear it. I'm also worried my ears may start bleeding.

When he looks out the window, I bend down to retie my combat boot and stick a teeny piece of film onto his briefcase. Most assassins would ditch the gun right away. The fact that he didn't either shows stupidity or extreme confidence, and I'm betting it's the latter. On the other hand, it could just be a prop.

As we come to a stop at the airport, he picks up his briefcase and stands. I blow him a kiss then grab my backpack off the floor and depart, as well. While he heads toward ticketing, I follow the route that employees of the airport take.

"I put a tracker on his bag," I say to Terrance. "Figure out where he's going. I need to change." I step into a restroom, go into a stall, and strip off the leather jacket, hanging it and the backpack on the hook.

I change into a microfiber business suit, pull off the eye makeup stickers, and quickly twist my hair into a severe bun. Then I stuff what's left in the backpack into a French designer tote, minus the gun and the disguise—dropping them into a trash receptacle on the way out. When I emerge from the restroom, I look completely different.

"He's purchasing a ticket," Terrance says into my ear. "Hang on. I'm hacked into the airline's database. Okay. He's going to Lyon."

"Which is a major train hub," I reply. "That's smart. From there he could go anywhere."

"Wait, shit," Terrance says.

"What?"

"Olivia—I mean, Plague—just found a passport photo for a man whose facial recognition has a ninety-two percent match. That man is flying to Nice. And get this, the flights depart just five minutes apart from adjacent gates."

"Is Ari going to make it here?"

"No, he got held up with the police. You're on your own."

"Buy me tickets for both flights. Huntley goes to Nice. Businesswoman goes to Lyon. How much time do I have?"

"The first one starts boarding in fifteen minutes."

"Merda," I curse as I run to the self check-in, scan the business woman's passport, check in with no bags for the flight, and then go through security. The only problem is I need to go through security as Huntley, too.

"Wait. Did he go through security twice? As two different people?" I ask Terrance.

"No, he didn't—wait. He's headed out the security exit. Hang on. He's in the restroom. Is he doing what you just did? Changing the way he looks?"

"Probably."

"Terrance, have you been watching to see if anyone else is following him? Have you seen any sign of surveillance?"

"No, we haven't."

"Me neither," I reply as the assassin comes out of the restroom wearing a different shirt, a more casual hairstyle, and minus the glasses.

"Terrance, we're going to have to make a call. Will he go to Nice or Lyon?"

"Lyon," Terrance guesses.

"Which flight leaves first?"

"Nice."

"Then that's where he's going. He'll be the last man

on the plane. I have to hurry." I run to the nearest bathroom, change into a designer dress that makes me look like a princess, topping it with an expensive leather embroidered bomber jacket and high heels. I remove the contacts, quickly apply makeup, and fill a clutch with a few essentials.

An announcement informs me that the flight to Nice is now boarding, so I make my way through security then breeze on the plane, never even looking in the assassin's direction.

ONCE ARI GETS checked into a five-star hotel, he gets updated by Terrance on the situation with Huntley. He wishes he could go help her, but the police requested he stay in town until tomorrow in case they need him for further questioning. And his hightailing it to the airport, playing Ares Von Allister or not, would have been deemed suspicious.

He changes clothes, tossing his blood-soaked ones away, and has a driver take him back to the car—and more importantly to his backpack filled with potential clues.

I SIP ON champagne and take selfies to kill time as the other passengers board. Once the plane is mostly full, save for a single first class seat in the aisle next to mine, final boarding is called.

I'm starting to get nervous. If I chose the wrong plane, we're screwed.

One of the flight attendants holds out a tabloid, which has side-by-side photos of me on it—one where I'm dancing with Lorenzo at the Queen's Ball and the other holding hands with Daniel at the President's swearing in. "Will you sign this?" she asks discreetly just as the assassin slips into the empty seat.

"But of course," I say in French, then sign *Huntley Von Allister* across the front, adding a heart over the I.

"Merci beaucoup," she says then turns to the assassin. "Monsieur Durand, may I offer you a glass of champagne?" I note he's using a very common surname, the equivalent to a Smith.

He starts to wave the attendant away, but then glances at me. "Actually, I will have a glass. It's not often I am so lucky to be seated by such a beautiful woman."

It's not so often I'm lucky enough to be seated next to the world's most deadly assassin.

My phone buzzes with a text.

Concierge: *Designer Marcus Latrobe confirms your appointment. He will greet you upon arrival and take you to lunch at his club, where he will sketch designs for you.*

"What brings you to Nice?" the assassin asks me. "You missed the Cannes Film Festival."

"I'm meeting a Parisian-based designer in Cannes. He's going to design a few gowns for me."

"Are you famous? Should I know you? You speak perfect French but look American."

"I am American. Do you speak English?" He nods. I roll my eyes and switch to English. "I'm really not famous. I've just been in the press lately due to dating a few high profile men."

"Such as?"

"Daniel Spear."

"The Olympic athlete?"

"And now the President's son. I usually fly charter, but when I got the call from the designer today, I had just enough time to get to the airport and get on this flight. Thankfully it's a quick flight, and I did not have to endure coach."

"Who is the other high profile man you date?" he asks.

"Well, we're more friends now, since the whole kidnapping thing."

"That's why you look familiar." He points his finger toward me. "You're the girl who was kidnapped with the Prince of Montrovia and refused to be interviewed by the press."

"I would prefer to forget the incident," I state, tightly closing my eyes and shuddering. "People were shot in front of me. While I'm grateful to have been rescued, part of me would have rather been fed to the sharks than to have witnessed such gruesomeness. There is no way I could ever speak of it to the press. The British agent was good at his job, that's all I will say."

"Before the incident, there were rumors you would become the next Princess."

I frown. "Yeah."

"I'm sorry if I'm intruding," he says sincerely.

"No, it's okay. The Prince—I mean, the King— seems to have taken the ordeal in stride. I have not. And the Prince's cousin who was killed was a friend of mine who had just gotten engaged. Her sister, Clarice, was so distraught, she relinquished her crown and moved back to France.

I study his face for any reaction to Clarice's name.

There is none, whatsoever.

I can see why he has the reputation he does. He is very calm and collected for someone who just committed two high-profile murders.

WE TALK THROUGH the entire flight, pausing only to listen to the announcements. The assassin known as The Priest tells me his name is Henri and that he's a retired real estate investor who moved to Cannes and took up selling local real estate to keep himself out of trouble. He even produces a business card with his full name, Henri Durand.

"My brother and I were considering a purchase on the French Riviera, maybe I'll call you next time we are in town."

When we land, I get a text.

Marcus Latrobe: *My dearest Huntley, I regret to inform you that a small fire broke out in my Paris studio, and I will be unable to meet you this afternoon as I must deal with the authorities and the laborers who were treated for smoke inhalation. My driver will pick you up as planned but I will not arrive until later this evening. Please accept my deepest apologies. We have lunch reservations at Les Bourges, and I suggest you go without me. It takes most people up to a year to even get a reservation and their food is quite divine. Because I am a founding member, you will be allowed access in my absence. Please enjoy yourself.*

Me: *I completely understand and will see you when you arrive. I'm looking forward to it and appreciate you taking time during your holiday to meet with me. And I will definitely keep the reservation.*

The assassin politely gestures for me to deplane ahead of him, and it goes against all my training to allow a man of his talent to follow me.

When I get to the terminal, I stop right in front of him and mutter, "Merda."

"What's wrong?" he asks.

I hold up my phone and roll my eyes. "I rush here on a moment's notice. I don't even have a change of clothing with me and now the designer is delayed. And he says I should go to some private club called Les Bourges by myself for lunch."

"You are uncomfortable dining alone?"

"No, not at all. I'm just"—I pout—"disappointed."

"It just so happens that I am also a member of the Les Bourges club."

"You are? Is it really that good? Am I going to look stupid being there alone? You know what, I'll just go shopping to kill the time. It was nice meeting you."

Then I turn my back on him and make my way out of the airport where I greet the driver holding a sign with my name on it. As the driver leads me to a car that's idling at the curb, I fight the urge to turn around to see where the assassin is. I know he's behind me, though. I can still feel his presence.

As I'm sliding into the backseat, his hand stops the door from closing. I may look like a rich girl whose biggest care in the world is lunch, but that doesn't mean inside I'm not ready to strike at any moment. And I am fully prepared.

But I want to kill him in his home.

I want him to feel violated.

His safe haven no more.

I want him down on his knees.

Begging for his life.

"Miss Von Allister, would you like a lunch companion? It seems my afternoon appointment was cancelled, as well. I can show you around the club."

He's living in plain sight just like me, I think. Deep cover but not hiding.

And I know I'm playing a very dangerous game.

I remind myself of my mission. Find out who hired him. Then kill him.

This isn't at all how I imagined things would go down when I came face-to-face with him again. My plan was to do what I was taught—alter my looks, my gait, my posture, pretend to be different people, and simply let him lead me home.

Instead, I offer him a ride.

THE ASSASSIN'S CAR is at the airport, so he declines my offer and meets me there.

The Les Bourges Club, which translated means *upper crust*, doesn't look like much from the outside. An old wooden door set in the middle of an orange stucco building is sandwiched by a tailor and a leather goods store a couple blocks from the harbor. There is no sign denoting the entrance, just gold numbers above the door. I step into an entry with worn wooden floors. A hostess greets me by name and says, "This way, please." She leads me down the hall past the dining room, where fashionably dressed people are crammed together at little tables, and to another wooden door. She opens it, waves her hand toward a set of stairs, and says, "Enjoy."

I glance upward, wondering what is awaiting me at the top. I am weaponless and in a horrible tactical position, totally exposed. If The Priest has any inkling that I am after him, he would be smart to meet me here. To send me up these stairs. I'd be easy to pick off.

I take a deep breath and remind myself that Huntley would love this place. And I will admit, I'd love to explore it with someone other than The Priest.

I clump up the stairs in my heels, announcing my presence, but gripping my bag tightly in my hand. With the metal spikes that adorn it, it could do some damage in a pinch.

At the top of the stairs, I am greeted by yet another hostess. "Monsieur Durand is waiting for you in the Spy Bar."

I gulp. The what!? *Did I hear her right?*

She leads me to a contemporary room that looks out of place in this old building. It features black and white marble floors, a stainless bar with Lucite stools, and red velvet walls covered with posters from every *007* movie ever made.

The assassin is seated on one of the stools chatting with a pretty bartender in a tight red dress. She sets a drink on the bar. "Your usual."

I sit down next to him.

"What would you like?" he says.

"A glass of champagne would be nice."

AFTER A LONG lunch at the club, where I manage to get the assassin a bit intoxicated, I offer him a ride.

This time, he accepts.

When my driver drops him off, I tag the location on my phone and am driven to the designer's home. I'm escorted to a bedroom where a suitcase awaits me.

I thank the butler and mention needing a nap.

Inside the suitcase are black yoga pants, a matching top, and a pair of black running shoes.

It reminds me of the uniform I wore during my six years at Blackwood.

I remember how M's face would light up when we would sneak out to the club and how she would dance with reckless abandon. I hope she's dancing her ass off somewhere now.

I drop to the bed and allow myself to cry.

I can't believe they are all dead.

Because of me.

I owe it to her—to all of them—to figure out what Black X is up to and why.

I pull myself together and continue to unpack the bag, finding a handgun buried under the clothing.

I get myself into mission mode by checking the gun, pulling the assassin's address up on the Internet, and studying the surrounding area. I need to be able to get in and out of there without being noticed.

Because it's a residential street and not more than a mile from where I am, I decide to walk rather than drive. I find a yoga studio just a block away and check their online schedule.

I glance at the clock.

I don't have much time.

I JOG AROUND the assassin's neighborhood before I approach his house. Google Earth is great for planning, but nothing can beat your own visual reconnaissance. I study the area, noting possible escape routes and problem zones. After doing my due diligence, I check out the assassin's back yard. Most of the homes in the city are row houses, but on this street and the one facing it, there are detached villas, each with their own fenced garden.

My original thought was to slip into the garden and break into the home, but that is fraught with risk. Especially during daylight hours. And although I was trained to quickly disable most security systems, I wouldn't want to try doing it with an assassin in the house.

So, I decide to just walk up to the front door and knock.

"Hey," he says, looking pleasantly surprised when he opens the door. "You out for a run?"

"Yeah. The designer was further delayed, so I decided

to take a yoga class and discovered the studio was just down the street from you. Class doesn't start for awhile, so I thought I'd stop by."

The assassin stands in the doorway, blocking the entrance and not allowing me inside. I was hoping not to have to force the issue.

"Um, sorry, it was rude of me to just stop by without calling first."

"No," he says. "I'm glad you did. Would you like to come in?"

His words are like music to my ears. "Yes, thank you. I would."

He steps aside.

I walk in.

He closes the door.

I reach for my revolver then spin toward him, gun leveled, causing his eyes go wide with astonishment.

"What are you doing?"

"Put your hands on top of your head and walk in the living room. No sudden movement, or you're dead."

He does as I ask.

"Get down on your knees."

Once again, he complies.

I now have the assassin exactly where I want him.

Exactly where I envisioned him all these years.

In the exact position he had my mother in—on his knees in front of me.

My gun pointed directly at his forehead.

"Tell me who hired you to kill the President," I demand, keeping both my focus and aim directed at him.

"Who sent you?" he asks. There's a slight tremble in his voice, something I hadn't expected. He had to know with his chosen profession that someday it would come to this.

"You killed the President of the United States. Did you really think you'd get away with it?"

"Yes, I've gotten away with every job I've ever been hired for. I am the best."

"Not this time," I say as my finger twitches against the trigger.

This is it. It's time.

I take a deep breath, wondering why I'm hesitating when a tiny voice behind me says, "Papa?"

My heart stops.

My throat goes dry.

My body stiffens.

I don't dare turn around.

"Please," the assassin begs, "not in front of my child."

His child?

Images of myself watching my mother in this exact position flash through my brain. Only this child sounds much younger than I was. Seeing his father's head blown off would warp him forever.

"You didn't offer that courtesy to my mother," I

reply, still remaining cool on the outside, even though internally I am panicking. I cannot allow a child to experience what I did.

"Your mother?" he asks, then a look of recognition crosses his face, and his hand involuntary goes to the scar on his arm.

"Don't move!" I yell. "Put your hands back on top of your head."

"Chauncey, don't do it!" the assassin yells.

I glance over my shoulder and see a boy of about six waving a gun in my direction.

Will this be my end?

Shot by the son of the man who killed my mother?

One lucky shot and boom, I'm gone from the world, and who would care?

Lorenzo, maybe, but he would soon seek comfort in another woman's arms. Daniel probably wouldn't even notice until he got horny. Ari would feel like he failed his mission, and that would be it.

The assassin gets up and takes the gun from his son. "If you were going to kill me, you would have already done it."

"I wanted you to know who I was first. I was sent by my government, but they gave me this job because I have been dreaming of this moment for the last six years."

"You have to believe me. I didn't know you were there until you shot me."

"And then you tried to kill me!"

"How did you find me?"

"I was given the location of your Paris hit and followed you. I blew you a kiss on the train, got rid of my disguise and got on the plane to Cannes as myself."

"That was you on the train? That was a good disguise."

"Thank you."

"You better get this over with then, and when you leave, please, take my son with you. We don't have much time."

"What do you mean?"

"If you know where I am, others do, too. There has been a bounty on my head for years. There is no doubt that they will be here soon."

"Papa?" the child says again.

He speaks to his son in French, telling him everything is all right and that he's proud of his bravery. When he wraps his arms around his son in a hug, there are tears in his eyes.

He believes it will be the last time he sees him.

"Do you feel it?" he says to me. "Can you feel the chaos coming our way?"

I do. And the sound of a helicopter in the distance isn't making me feel any better.

"Where should we go?"

"Set of stairs leading to an underground tunnel," he

says, pointing to a bookcase. "You have two options. Kill me, take the credit, and earn the bounty. Or—"

"Or what?"

"Don't let my son see what you saw. I'm sorry. I wouldn't have wished that on any child. Please, take him far away from here. Leave me for them."

The chopper is getting closer. I quickly run all possible scenarios through my head and come to a decision.

"There's a third option."

"What's that?"

"You come with us."

"How could you ever trust me?"

"How could you trust me with your son?"

"Because you don't have the eyes of a cold-blooded killer. They're getting closer," he says.

"Then I'm in danger, too. We could fight them together and win, but it would be difficult to protect your son during the battle. And we won't know how many of them there are."

"They will come in full force. I've killed too many men to send just one."

"What if we had a surprise for them?"

"Like what?"

"If they are coming in force, I assume they will shoot first and ask questions later. Do you have a gas stove?"

The assassin smiles at me. A smile that spreads to his eyes. Eyes that hold the joy of fatherhood.

I tuck my pistol in the back of my pants, grab his son, and carry him down the stairs. "Stay here. We'll be right back," I say to him in French, then I run up to the kitchen.

The Priest now has an assault rifle, but it's hanging loosely across his body.

"Let's help it along." I open his pantry, but don't find what I'm looking for, so I open the refrigerator and find a metal take-out container. I throw it in the microwave and then slam the door shut, as the sounds of the chopper get louder. They are almost directly above us now.

Knowing we don't have much time before things get ugly, I set the microwave for two minutes and hit *start* as The Priest turns on the burner, then blows out the flame.

We both run to the bookcase and down the stairs. He picks his son up, kisses him, then pushes him into my arms. "Go."

"Come with me!" It takes everything I have to not feel like a child myself. Even though I hate him, I don't want him to die right now.

"Please, go," he begs. "I will follow if I am able."

I wrap my arms around the child, kiss his forehead, and tell him to hold tight. Then I run as fast as I can down the dark tunnel with one arm out, praying I don't crash into anything. The tunnel is a straight shot, and I've traveled a very short distance when I come to another set of stairs.

"Stay here," I say, trying to set him down. But the boy clings to me, shaking his head, obviously scared.

"Promise you won't make a peep?"

He doesn't reply, just nods his little head.

I take a deep breath, grab the pistol from my back, and aim it in front of us as I silently traverse up the stairs. Just like in The Priest's home, there is a wooden door at the top. I open it, peeking out of a matching bookcase in the front room of a similar home.

There are sheer curtains covering the windows, but I can clearly make out an assault team—dressed in black military garb, their faces covered—as they rappel down from the sky. One team of four moves into position in front of the house, the other takes the back. I briefly wonder if this is how many they will send some day when I'm through serving my usefulness.

Of course, I work for my country, not for the highest paying bidder.

The helicopter has a military look but no identifying marks. The only things of consequence are the matching PP-19 Bison submachine guns the men are carrying, which are favored by the Russian Spetsnaz, their special forces.

I look back down the stairs, hoping to find The Priest coming to tell me the rest of his escape plan as the men's boots hit the ground, and they start firing in unison at the house.

I hear a whoosh.

Knowing what's coming next, I hurl my body on top of the boy as the air flashes orange and the house across the street explodes into a fireball.

The detonation blows out the windows of the house we're in and sucks all the air out.

I'm struck in the side by the bookcase door swinging back at me with force.

"Ugh," I yell, as pain rips through my side.

THE AIR IS thick with the smell of burning wood, and I can hear the crackling of flames.

Through everything, the boy has been silent, but now he starts sobbing softly, his big brown eyes filled with tears.

Once I determine he's not injured, I pick him up and hug him.

He clings to me, not wanting to let go.

Tears stream down my face as I tighten our embrace.

The fact that his father has not joined us is a bad sign. And even though this is what I wanted, what I prayed for—the assassin dead—I instantly wish I could take it back.

Lorenzo was right. Revenge doesn't bring back the dead. It only further adversely affects the living.

Just like it will affect this little boy for the rest of his life.

Now he's an orphan just like me.

And it's all my fault.

THE DISTANT SOUND of sirens takes me out of my reverie. I set the boy down and tell him to stay put, then I move stealthily across the glass-strewn living room to survey what's going on next door.

The house is destroyed.

The helicopter must have gotten in the way of the explosion, caught fire, and crashed into the street. The house is in shambles and on fire, smoke and ash billowing from it. The assault team was close to the explosion. Even though they were wearing body armor, I doubt any survived.

I watch as a neighbor rushes to what's left of them, checking for a pulse on one who is mostly intact.

I want to run next door and check the rubble for The Priest.

I want to search for clues as to who sent the assault team.

But I can't.

We need to go.

I run back to the stairs and grab the boy's hand.

"What's your name?" he asks in French.

I tell him it's Huntley. I'm not sure where I'm going to take him, but I have to get this child somewhere safe.

Somewhere far away from here.

More than likely, whoever sent these men will be sending a clean-up crew to dispose of evidence of their involvement.

Not to mention the police and rescue teams that are already on their way.

"I'm Chauncey," the boy says. He has dark hair, big brown eyes, and eyelashes so long and thick you'd think he had extensions.

"How old are you?"

"I'm six."

"We have to go on a trip," I tell him.

"Trip!" he exclaims. He pulls out of my grip, runs into the small kitchen, and points to the pantry.

Curious, I open the door.

Inside are two backpacks. One sized for a child, and one an adult pack.

He puts his on, so I grab the other and sling it over my shoulder. He takes my hand and leads me out the back door and down the alley until we arrive at a park.

I expect him to want to play, but curiously, he takes me across the street and points out a bar. "We have to go there."

I think about the song Lorenzo's grandfather taught him to help him escape the castle in a time of danger. About how my parents told me to go to Uncle Sam's if I was ever in trouble. Is that what this is? Did his father train him to do the same—with or without him?

As we enter the dark bar, I grip the boy's hand tightly.

There are only a few patrons, but they all turn their heads in our direction.

So, I ask where the bathroom is. Who can turn down a kid who has to pee?

The bartender gestures toward the back. I keep my head down and lead the boy that way.

WHEN WE GET into the bathroom, I ask Chauncey if he needs to use the restroom. He shakes his head no, so I set him up on the counter and have him wash his hands while I open his backpack.

A sound behind me causes me to stop.

I turn to see the bartender approaching in a menacing way. When he places his hand on my shoulder and grips it tightly, I grab his hand and spin, sweeping my leg across the man's kneecap and causing him to fall to the ground.

I pull the pistol out of my waistband and take aim.

"Was the explosion for his father?"

"Yes," I say, the gun trained on him. "Do you know what he does for a living?"

"The boy has his special backpack," the bartender replies. "That means he is on the run. Why are you with him? Although, that is a stupid question based on the way you just handled yourself. Are you in the same line of work?"

"No, I'm just a friend. A scared friend." I pretend shake then let the gun fall to my side. "I'm sorry about your leg. It's the only move I know."

I put the gun away and help the man up.

"In the boy's backpack are travel documents. Passport. Birth certificate," he says.

"Are they real?"

"Yes, but there are two additional sets of forged ones in the other pack. Tell me what happened."

"A helicopter was coming. He sent us down a tunnel and over to the other house. Military men with machine guns came down from the sky." I purposefully name their weapon incorrectly. "They fired at the house and then it exploded. I got scared. Told the boy we were going on a trip. He got the backpacks and brought me here."

"You're a bright lad," he says, ruffling the boy's hair. "Your papa would be proud." Then he turns to me. "You will care for him?"

"What about his mother?" I ask in English, hoping he understands.

The little boy surprises me by speaking in English. "Momma with angels."

My heart skips a beat.

"How?" I ask.

"In a hit that was meant for him. Four years ago. That is when we came here."

"Are you related?"

"Old friends. We started out in the military together."

"Are you in the same line of business?"

"I brokered his jobs."

I let out a sigh. "Okay, I lied before. I am in the same line of work and was sent here to kill him. We were able to get the location of the hit in Paris. I followed him home. It's only a matter of time before they discover the location of your computer—if they haven't already. You're in danger, too."

"I have my own escape plan. You must leave now with the boy and get him somewhere safe. Can you do that?"

"Yes, I can," I say, remembering that Lorenzo was traveling to his home in London today and knowing that's where I need to go.

The man gives us both hugs, leads us to a back door, and hands me a set of keys. "Take my car."

"Thank you," I say.

Once I get the boy and the bags loaded up, the bartender slams me against the car. "If you think I'm going to let you take the boy, you're wrong." He pulls a gun on me and shoves it into my temple.

"Put the gun away, please. You're going to scare the

child. I should know. Six years ago, The Priest shot and killed my mother in front of me."

The bartender backs away in shock. "*You* are the girl who shot him? Who escaped from him?"

"Yes, I am. And I've been training since then. I was sent here for retribution—for my mother and for the President of the United States, but I couldn't do it. Not with his son there—probably not at all."

"Then I understand why he allowed you to take the boy. You will fiercely defend him, won't you?"

"Yes," I say, then break down, the tears I've been trying to hold in coming at me like a tidal wave.

"You are a beautiful young woman," he says solemnly. "Forget about this life. Take the boy and retire. In the backpack is a key to a safety deposit box in Zurich. There is enough money for whatever you could possibly need. Give him a normal life."

"There were two parts to my mission. One was to find out who ordered the hits."

"I can't tell you."

"But you don't understand. I can't possibly have a normal life unless I find out."

"If I tell you, do you promise to take care of the boy?"

"You have my word."

He contemplates this for a few seconds. "Normally, I do not know who hires us. That is part of the business.

Someone orders a hit. The hit is completed. Money is wired. It is all done covertly, anonymously. We don't care who hires us or their reason for it—only that we are paid."

"So you don't know?"

"At first he turned down the hit on the President. The job was too big and not worth the risk. Then a message came back with a higher offer and something more important. Information. Six years ago, after he took the hit on your mother, he was double-crossed. A team of men was sent to kill him and he and his family barely escaped. We learned the man who ordered that hit was John Hillford, Senior."

"But how could that be? My mother worked for the government!"

"I don't know why. And I don't know who ordered the hit on the President. It came through a middleman. The money man."

"I need to know his actual name."

"Fine," he says, quickly sprawling the name across my hand. "But I must warn you. He is a very bad man." The bartender hugs me. "Please, you must go now."

I get into the car in stunned silence, putting the key in the ignition and starting the car.

When I do, I notice my watch.

I pull it off, not wanting to be tracked, and hand it to the bartender. I explain how it works and tell him that there is a tracking device in it.

He nods in understanding. "I'll take care of this for you. Now, go." He pats the top of the car as we drive off.

ONCE WE ARE out of town, I stop and call my emergency number.

"Is your mission complete?" the distorted voice asks.

"Yes. The Priest is dead. I killed him. But while I was still in his house a team of eight men rappelled out of a military chopper. Thankfully, I heard the chopper coming and prepared. When they started firing, the house exploded and the men perished. I was lucky to have escaped."

"Did you put metal in the microwave and turn on the gas, like you were taught?"

"Yes, I did."

"Good girl."

"Were the men sent to kill me?"

"They were not." The Dean's true voice comes on the line. "I suspect that others may have discovered the whereabouts of the assassin and sent a team."

"Because they are tracking me?"

"No—they don't know about you."

"Well, I'm lucky to have escaped. I'll be taking a few days off. Going off grid."

"Back to Montrovia?"

"Honestly, it's none of your business."

"We can track your phone."

"I know. That's why I'm throwing it out the window as soon as I end this call. I just killed my mother's assassin. I need some time to figure out if I want to continue in this line of work."

"Just remember, X. The assassin may have killed your mother, but someone hired him to do so. You must find out who ordered the hit."

"I already know the answer to that. It was John Hillford, Senior."

"What?" he replies with shock. "That can't be."

"Well, it is. What I want to know is why the government my mother worked for wanted her dead."

"You know?"

"Yes, I know that my mother worked for the CIA. And I know you've been lying to me. Goodbye." I toss the phone out of the window.

"Where are we going?" the boy asks.

"London," I reply.

"Yipee!" He claps. "Does that mean we can get bangers and mash?"

"Absolutely."

I DRIVE AIMLESSLY, making sure I'm not being followed.

My mind is numb.

Not only did I not complete my mission, I am now responsible for a child. On a positive note, I did discover who ordered the hit on my mother and the name of the money man.

Before I threw my phone away, I memorized three important people's numbers: William Gallagher—AKA Intrepid, Juan, and Mike Burnes. I contemplate who I should call.

As long as I'm in France, I don't have to worry about being found. We can cross most European borders without showing our passports—unless the rules suddenly change, and with the recent terrorist attacks in France that could happen at any minute.

Telling the Dean that I need time to think will buy me a few days off. After that, I think they will come looking for me. Someone has invested too much time, money, and blood in me. They won't allow me to quit.

They will kill me first.

The fact that they were able to get Ari and I transported to France on a fighter jet, says whomever I am working for has serious clout.

But first things first.

I need to get the child somewhere safe.

Then I need to return to Montrovia as Huntley and keep pretending.

I'm starting to come down from the adrenaline rush that's been going since we set foot on the airbase. I pull off the side of the road, park the car, and close my eyes for a few moments. Just as I start to drift to sleep, I remember the backpacks.

I open my eyes with a start and grab them from the backseat, careful not to wake the boy, who dozed off.

Starting with the boy's pack, I discover a passport for Chauncey Durand. There are a couple changes of clothing, a stuffed tiger, a soft blanket, and a photo of a woman holding the boy when he was about two. In another pouch, there are typical travel items—snacks and a tablet loaded with video games along with a set of headphones.

In the bigger pack, I find the two additional sets of passports along with corresponding credit cards, a buck knife, a handgun with spare clips, two grenades, three throwaway cell phones, a charger, a wad of Euros, and the key to the safety deposit box in Zurich.

I study the key, realizing it looks familiar—exactly like the one I retrieved from Blackwood.

Which is in my handbag along with my Huntley Von Allister passport.

I DRIVE THE ten kilometers back to Cannes. I can still see the smoke rising over the boy's house. When I arrive at the designer's home, I park the car just down the street and wake the boy up.

"Papa?" he says, then he sees me and smiles. "Are we there yet?"

"Not yet. I have to pick up my bag." I grab the tablet

from the backpack and hand it to him. "If you promise to stay in the car, I'll let you play a game."

"Angry Birds?" he asks with a grin.

"Yes, you can play whatever you want. I'll be right back."

I crack the windows, take the keys, and lock the boy in the car. Since I'm still wearing workout clothes, I jog up the street, taking note of a black SUV. I drop down behind a hedge, following it around to the side of the designer's cottage, where I left the French door to the terrace unlocked.

Not ready to commit yet, I sneak back to check on the SUV. As I pop my head up from the hedge, I see a man wearing a captain's hat pulling a wheeled suitcase down the driveway, followed by a distinguished looking elderly woman.

I let out a sigh of relief, thankful it's not an assault team searching for me.

I run back to the house, sneak in the door, retrieve my bags without incident, and race back to the car.

THE BOY IS still where I left him, happily playing his game. I grab one of the phones, call Juan, and ask to speak to Lorenzo.

"Are you safe?" he asks.

"Lorenzo, are you in London?" I ask, trying to keep the panic out of my voice. I just lied to one of the most elite covert operations in the world. I have to be very careful about what I say and do next.

"Yes, we arrived this afternoon. Where are you?" He lowers his voice. "And are you safe?"

I know what he's asking. And even though no one can trace this burner because I'll be tossing it out the window the second I finish the call, I don't know who's listening in on his end. It probably wouldn't surprise Black X if I took a few days off to be with the Prince, but I don't dare say anything else.

"Yes, I am. Where are you staying?"

"We have a lovely place in Notting Hill."

"Could you text the address to this number?"

"Of course, and I shall be awaiting your arrival on bated breath."

"Lorenzo, I'll be there late. Will you meet me alone?"

"Of course, my darling," he replies. I feel bad for giving him the wrong impression, but I didn't have a choice.

I have no idea what I'll tell him when I get there. Or, quite frankly, how I'm going to get there.

I toss the phone out the window, make sure the boy is buckled in, and drive north toward Le Cannet.

Then I use another burner phone.

"Gallagher," he answers.

"This is bag girl, I need your help."

"You must have the wrong number." He hangs up

on me.

I hold my phone out in front of me, staring at it, not sure what to do.

When he doesn't call back, I tell the boy we're going to drive for a while.

"Can I keep playing my game?" he asks.

"For as long as you want."

A FEW MINUTES LATER, the phone rings.

"It's Gallagher. I wasn't in a secure environment," he explains when I answer. "I don't know if you've heard the reports, but the assassin who killed the President is dead."

"I heard that," I say. "However, there was a complication. I may need you to, like, smuggle me and possibly someone else into your country."

"You couldn't do it, could you? Did you kidnap him instead? Did you lie about his death?"

"I don't have a lot of time to explain. Can you help me?"

"Where are you?"

"Close to where he was killed. Where are you?"

"Monaco."

"Vacation?"

"I brought our mutual friend here."

"Can I meet you?"

"Go to the Colline du Chateau in Nice. Walk

around the grounds. I'll find you."

"I'll be there in less than an hour."

I check the road signs ahead and see that the A8 autoroute, known as La Provencale, is a few miles ahead, which will take me northwest toward Nice.

"I'm hungry," the boy says, looking up from his game. "Are we in London yet?"

"No, we are going to see a castle. Have you ever seen one?"

"I've been to many castles. I want to be a knight when I grow up. Knights protect the people."

What he says makes me smile. "Want to hear a secret?"

"Yes, I'm good at keeping secrets."

"I'm a knight."

"Girls can't be knights."

"They can if they are very brave."

"I'm very brave," he says.

"I know you are. You knew to get the backpacks and took me to see your daddy's friend."

"That was our escape route. You only take the escape route when things are bad. My house exploded. That was bad."

"Yes, it was. I'm going to take you somewhere else to live."

"While Daddy is on his trip?"

"Yeah," I say. "While Daddy is on his trip."

The boy nods in understanding, puts his head back down, and focuses on his game. I stare at his little dark head and pray I can pull this off without getting us killed.

WE ARRIVE IN Nice, park near the beach, and then walk up the stairs to the castle, stopping to view the waterfall and lookout along the way. I took a bottle of water and some snacks out of his backpack, and he's happily chomping away and running through the ruins of the castle. I curiously watch as he sneaks around the edge of a doorway, his fingers forming a gun, then pops out and pretends to shoot. I wonder just what other skills his father taught him.

A memory flashes in my brain. The painful kind that I usually block, but this one comes at me with too much force. My mother is trying to take a photo of me, but I keep popping behind the castle wall, hiding, then leaning my head around the corner and sticking my tongue out at her. *"You should let me take your picture, Lee,"* she says, *her voice like music to my ears. "I want you to always remember our visit to the Palacio de la Vallenta."*

"Huntley," Intrepid says, startling me.

I frantically scan the ruins for the boy, quickly spotting him, still playing. I take a deep breath and rub my hands down my face.

"You look tired," he says. "Who is the boy?"

"His son."

"*The Priest's* son?"

"Yes."

It's Intrepid's turn to rub his face. "Bloody hell. I just got rid of one of your problems, now you bring me the assassin's son?"

"I just need you to get us to London. I'll hire a nanny and hide him at Lorenzo's place there."

"I can't do that. *You* can't do that."

"I promised I would, but I understand if you can't help. I'll make other arrangements. Thanks for coming."

I stand up and walk away.

"Playtime is over, Chauncey. Let's hit the road again."

"Okay," he says, slipping his little hand into mine and squeezing it. "Even though I want bangers and mash, we need go to Zurich. That's where I'm supposed to go next when things get bad."

"You're right," I say, thinking about my own key. "Let's go there."

"I know how to sign my name," he says as we're walking away.

"That's good," I reply, finding his comment very random.

"Daddy says you have to be able to sign your name to use a credit card," he finishes. And I realize I might just be able to do this on my own. Zurich is only six hours by car, and if we drive, I don't have to worry about using my passport. The kid is smart.

Intrepid is waiting for us at the bottom of the steps. "Fine. I'll do it."

I turn to the boy. "What is in Zurich?"

"Safety net," he answers.

"Feel like going for a ride with us first?" I ask.

"Where are we going?"

"To a bank in Switzerland."

I get the boy loaded into the car and turn it on to get the air-conditioning going.

"Why Switzerland?" he asks.

"He has a safety deposit box there. He knows how to sign his name and what to do. He says it's his safety net."

"It's too dangerous to take him now. Word is getting out about his father's death. They could be watching the account."

"I don't think anyone knows about it. And the faster we move, the better. Before someone does figure it out, we'll have the box emptied and will be gone. We can open the boy another account in London or, better yet, Montrovia. There's a phone number on the key. We have to let them know we are coming, particularly after hours."

"How do you know that?" he asks.

I blink a few times, thinking about my own key. "I'm not sure, but I know."

"Let's wait until we are there to call," he suggests. "And I'm driving. How long has it been since you've slept?"

"About thirty-six hours, maybe. I think I napped a little on the fighter jet."

"Fighter jet?"

"We had to get from D.C. to Paris in under four hours to be there in time for The Priest's next hit."

"I don't know who the hell this Black X group is, but they have serious military pull to make that happen."

"Maybe they aren't a covert spy agency. Maybe they have ties to the military. Ari's father was an important general."

"There isn't such a thing."

"There could be. A form of special forces, maybe?"

Intrepid nods his head. "Nothing would surprise me at this point."

I GET INTO the backseat with the boy. We pick up dinner and eat in it the car, then the boy lays his head on my lap, curls up into a little ball, and falls to sleep. I push his hair back off his forehead, running my fingers through it, as I lean my head against the window.

FIVE HOURS LATER, I wake up with a start when the car comes to a stop. A glance at the clock tells me it's nearly midnight.

"I tried calling the number on the key," Gallagher says. "It's not a working number, so I figured we'd just show up."

I wake Chauncey and tell him we're in Zurich.

"Excellent," he says, rubbing his eyes as I discreetly slip my own key out of my handbag.

"Are you ready to sign your name?"

He hops out of the car and leads us to the front of the sleek marble building with only a gold sign with the words *Z Investments* giving any indication that we are at a bank.

"I don't have to sign my name here, silly," he says, putting his index finger on a little glass circle under the placard.

The door clicks, and a man dressed in a suit greets us. "Do you have your key?" he asks in Swiss German.

Chauncey replies in the same language and then walks across the room. He comes to a door behind the reception desk and places his finger on another circle of glass, causing it to open.

I start to follow him, but the banker says to me in English, "The key holder must enter alone."

"I have one, too," I reply, speaking in his native tongue and causing Intrepid to narrow his eyes at me.

"Very well," the man says. "After the door closes, scan your fingerprint. I will take your companion to the exit lounge where he will await you."

I scan my fingerprint, go through the door, and find Chauncey already inserting his key into a box. I walk straight to the back wall and touch box number six twelve, then shake my head, looking at the key to determine which one is mine.

"Six twelve," my mom's voice says. "Your birthday." I close my eyes, concentrating, trying to hold onto the memory, trying to remember when I was here before, but the boy clanks his box on the table, and the memory is gone.

I watch as Chauncey pulls out a leather pouch, puts it in his backpack, and then returns the box. "Ready?" he asks.

"Wait for me, okay?" I mimic his actions and am removing the box from the wall when we hear gunfire.

"Shit." I stuff the metal container into the backpack, not bothering to look at its contents.

"Sounds like trouble out front. Do you have your gun?"

"I don't," I reply. "I left it in the car."

He reaches in his backpack, opens the leather pouch, and pulls out a Glock. "I'm not a very good shot yet. Are you? If you are truly a knight, you should be."

We hear shouting then more shots fired.

"There's a secret exit, Huntley. Only accessible by fingerprint." He points toward a door. "William will be waiting for us there. Go get him."

"You're kind of bossy," I say. "Definitely knight material."

I do as the kid says, but the door won't budge.

"I think some people might be after us."

"Then we'd better hurry." He runs to the back corner of the room with me hot on his tail.

There is one long blast from an automatic weapon and the shooting stops.

We hear a voice yell out, "Clear!"

"They're trying to blow the door to the vault," I yell. "Hurry, Chauncey!"

The boy presses his finger against the wall, causing a door to slide open. We enter the next room, the door slides shut, and we find ourselves in a soundproofed tunnel.

The tunnel is about one hundred feet long then comes to a dead end. The boy places both his palms against the wall and a screen lights up, showing us security feeds. This allows us to see the assault team, all dressed in black and carrying the same weapons as the men who came after The Priest. I want to believe that they are just robbers and we chose an unfortunate time to visit the bank, but I know better.

The question is, which one of us caused them to come?
Me or the boy?

I study the monitors more closely, searching for Gallagher. But I can't find him anywhere.

Please, don't let him be dead.

"I can't remember what to do next," Chauncey says. "Do you know?"

I lean my head against the wall in defeat. I have no idea how we're going to get out of here, but I need to stay positive for the boy, so I put my hands on the wall and push myself upright. "I don't know, but we'll figure it out."

Suddenly, a series of numbers flashes by.

Then my mother appears on the screen and speaks. "If you are seeing this message, Lee, you are in grave danger. This account includes a safe passage clause, but use your best judgment. Bankers can be bought."

The screen turns black and a wall to our right opens to reveal another passage.

"Is your mommy an angel, too?" the boy whispers.

"Stay behind me," I tell him, not answering the question as I hide the Glock behind my back and prepare for the worst.

ARI TAKES A private plane from Paris to Montrovia. Ellis is there to pick him up when he arrives.

"Have you heard from Huntley?" he asks.

"When she called in to report the completion of her mission, she was told to take a few days off. You probably could use some R&R as well."

"I'm afraid I don't have time for that. Terrance is

supposed to be meeting me here."

"He is in the basement awaiting your arrival," Ellis replies. "He said you may be down there for a while, so I have fully stocked it with food and caffeinated beverages."

"Thank you."

ONCE IN THE basement, Ari lays out everything he found at Clarice's home on a table. Terrance suggests starting with the phone, so they listen to the messages from her boyfriend, Armend.

Since she'd moved back to Paris and renounced her claim to the throne, she had been avoiding him. He was upset about it. By the last message, he had gone from desperate to mad and then back to desperate again.

But none of what he says seems to relate to her being in danger or her knowing anything about her sister's plan to overthrow the monarchy of Montrovia.

The same is true of her recent call list and her contact list. All are checked and double-checked, but still lead nowhere.

While Terrance starts sifting through the files on her computer, Ari uses her phone to check all of her social media sites. An easy task, since she was already logged on.

Ari reads her profiles and posts, going back a year, and checks all of her messages.

"This is useless," he says, slamming down the phone and feeling frustrated.

"Going through all of this requires much patience," Terrance says, looking up from the computer. "Take a break if you need to. Go work out or something. Clear your head. Sometimes it's not until later that you realize you passed over something of importance. When you get back, why don't you start on the diary? At least that should make for interesting reading."

I MOVE STEALTHILY down the dark passageway, the boy following me. We come to another dead end, this one, we can't find a way out of. I press on the walls, as does the boy, but nothing happens.

I search my mind, but can't recall anything, my memories seemingly walled off and surrounded by a moat.

I try everything, putting both hands on each wall. Looking for a hidden lever. A hidden door.

Anything.

The good news is no one seems to be coming after us. The bad news is no one seems to be coming to help us either.

I think about the explosives that were used on the door to the safety deposit box room. There are a couple of grenades in the backpack. I've thought about trying to blast our way out, but I fear they would not have the desired effect of taking out an exterior wall, but rather would explode down the tunnel, killing us both.

"That's it," I say aloud. "Maybe there's a trap door. Like at your house."

I drop to my hands and knees and knock on the floor, hoping there is something below the carpet.

Suddenly, the room shakes violently. Although we couldn't hear it, we could definitely feel another blast.

They are blowing their way through the tunnels and vaults, trying to get to us.

I rip up the carpet and place both my palms on the floor; which then lights up and causes a trap door to pop open.

Feeling both relief as well as an odd sense of deja vu, the boy and I climb down the ladder and come to a steel door. Chauncey touches a visible screen to the right, causing it to unlatch and open. I jump in front of him, my gun at the ready.

We are now in a subterranean concrete garage, subtly lit with pale purple lights, where a fleet of vehicles awaits us.

There is a rack of keys on the wall in front of me with a number corresponding to the parking spots. I move the child behind a concrete pillar and fire the gun at a Bugatti Veyron, thrilled when the bullet ricochets and the window remains in tact.

Apparently safe passage equals armored cars.

I grab a set of keys, load the child in the front seat, and tell him to get strapped in. Although he'd be safer in a car with a backseat, I need something fast to get us out of here, and even fully armored it will double the top speed of anything that would have brought an assault team. It will even outrun a helicopter.

As I slide into the lush cockpit of the beautiful and outrageous car, I feel like Huntley Von Allister. No one will suspect this car is carrying a trained killer and the son of the world's most infamous one.

As we emerge from the underground garage, a few blocks from the entrance to the bank, we hear sirens. I know I shouldn't, but I can't help it. I need to know.

There are two SUVs parked at an angle in front of the bank, their doors still open. I don't see anyone in the trucks as I drive by, so I roll down the window and toss a grenade under each one, then stomp on the accelerator.

We're a block away when the vehicles explode behind us.

"Woah," Chauncey says, looking back. "That was awesome! Just like the movies!"

"And it should keep them busy for awhile," I agree, smiling at him.

ONCE WE ARE a safe distance away, I pull over, take a deep breath, and pray that Intrepid managed to escape.

"Can we get hot cocoa?" Chauncey asks. "Daddy

always makes it for me before bed."

There are no shops open, so I tell him that I will make him some with extra chocolate as soon as we get to London.

He nods, still clutching the backpack tightly to his chest. Although he was calm and collected at the bank, he now looks rattled and scared. I unbuckle myself and take his bag.

"Let's put this on the floor," I say, handing him the stuffed tiger.

He hugs the tiger then promptly falls asleep.

I have one throwaway phone left, but don't want to use it yet.

Instead, I grab the boy's iPad, find free Wi-Fi at a nearby nightclub, and pull up a map of the area, searching for the closest airstrip. There is a military base ten kilometers southeast, a small airport—one that apparently has a good on-site restaurant—six kilometers to the east, and about ten other options within a fifty kilometer radius.

I choose the one I would have chosen if I were in charge of the mission planning.

Thirty minutes later, for what should have been a ten-minute trip, we arrive at the airport—the delay caused by me doubling back twice to make certain we weren't being followed.

As we get close, I spot a plane with the call sign G-MISX. The first letter indicating the plane's home country of Britain, and I pray the rest stands for MI6, the British Intelligence Agency that Intrepid works for.

I pull the car up to airport's gated entrance. A man with an automatic weapon and wearing the uniform of the British Royal Air Force steps out of the guard stand, his gun trained on us.

"This is a secure location. Please move away," he threatens.

"I'm looking for William Gallagher."

"I'm afraid I don't know who you're talking about," the soldier replies. "Please depart the premises or risk arrest."

"What about the MI6 agent whose code name is Intrepid. Do you know him? You're a British soldier on foreign land. We are why you are here. We were just with Intrepid at a Swiss bank. An assault team came in. We managed to escape, but we don't know if he did."

"Please stay here," the soldier says, going back to the guard stand while still keeping his gun trained on us.

A few moments later, soldiers surround the car, their guns drawn.

The good news is that they probably don't know this car is armored. I could hit reverse, flip a cookie, and hightail it out of here.

But then what?

Where would I go?

If I were by myself, I'd go back to the bank to look for Intrepid, but it's too risky with the boy. I can't put him in any more danger.

What if these men are the bad guys? What if their uniforms are a ruse?

"Get buckled, Chauncey. Now," I whisper. "We may have to get out of here fast."

"Are they going to shoot at us?" he cries. "I want my daddy."

"I do, too," I say, putting the car into reverse and readying my foot on the accelerator.

"What is your code name?" one of them asks.

"It's either Bag Girl or X," I reply.

"She's clear," he yells out then turns back to us. "Please, come follow me."

I nod, tears of relief filling my eyes as I put the car in park and turn it off.

"Don't cry," Chauncey says as he gets himself un-buckled. "We're all right now."

When he gets out of the car, he leaps into my arms.

"You're right," I say, giving him a squeeze. "We're safe now."

An airman takes our bags and carries them onto the plane.

"I heard you are very brave," he says, saluting

Chauncey.

"I'm going to be a knight someday," the boy tells him.

"What's your name?" the airman asks.

"Chauncey."

"Sir Chauncey, I like it. Would you like to meet the pilots and see the cockpit while we wait for our other passenger?"

The boy leaps out of my arms and follows him, suddenly having a new best friend. He checks out the plane, shakes the hands of the pilots, and comes back with a pair of aviation wings pinned to his shirt.

"I'm hungry," he says, making himself at home in one of the seats. "Are we going to London for bangers and mash now?"

"Yes, we are."

A steward offers the boy some biscuits and jam, which he happily accepts. "Do you have any hot chocolate?"

The steward smiles and makes him a cup of cocoa from a mix.

"Have you heard from Gallagher?" I ask. "Do you know if he's okay?"

"He's a little worse for wear, but he's okay," a voice says from behind me.

I turn around and see him. He's a mess. His suit is tattered and covered in dust.

I rush to him, throwing my arms around his neck.

"I was very worried about you two," he says. "Particularly when the explosives were detonated."

"What happened?"

"I was escorted to the room where you would exit from when you had concluded your business. But things got a little dodgy when gunmen came in. The receptionist hit a silent alarm, which then shut off that exit to you, meaning they couldn't get to you, but neither could I. Two men came in back. I took them out."

"Were they bank robbers?" I ask hopefully.

He shakes his head. "They were after one of you. There must have been a message sent out as soon as the fingerprint was scanned, because the response was almost immediate."

"You look like you could use this, sir," the steward says, handing Gallagher a drink.

One of the pilots steps out of the cockpit. "We just got a call from the gate where there is an unidentified, unfriendly vehicle. You may have been followed here. We can fight it out or take off."

"Let's get the hell out of here, now!" Gallagher replies.

We get buckled up, taxi down the runway, and quickly ascend.

I hold my breath, half waiting for the plane to be shot out of the sky.

Once we're safely airborne, I let it out.

Intrepid is sitting next to me. He lays his hand on top of mine and nods toward Chauncey, who is chewing a bit of biscuit with his eyes closed, trying to fight off sleep.

"Cute kid," he says.

"Smart kid. You should have seen him at the bank. He'd been there before. And I think I have been there, too. I had a couple of flashbacks today. My memories have been, um, iffy, I guess you could say, since my mom died. I remember a lot from when I was young but the time around her death, I can't remember."

"You can't remember or you don't want to?"

"I'm not sure there is a difference anymore. Now, I wish I could remember, but it's like my memories are encrypted or something."

"Trauma can cause that."

"So I've heard," I say with an eye roll.

"What was in the safety deposit boxes?"

"I don't know." I tell him all that happened on our end.

Once we reach cruising altitude, the steward gets up and folds out one of the seats, making up a bed. Then he unbuckles the boy and lays him down on it.

The boy wakes up and motions for me, so I sit on the floor next to him, rub his face, and wish him sweet dreams as he falls back to sleep.

"Can I make up a bed for either of you?" the steward asks.

"How long is the flight?"

"Ninety minutes," he replies.

"No, thank you. I'm fine."

I grab my backpack and pull out the safety deposit box.

Inside I find just four things. The first is another key, this one for a safety deposit box at the Royal Montrovian Bank. The second is a letter from my mother telling me that she was a covert agent, that she's sorry she couldn't tell me, how much she loves me, and how she hopes that I remember all the fun we had traveling together. The third item is a photo. The one I remembered today. I'm sticking my tongue out at her, peeking around the side of Lorenzo's castle. And lastly, there is a stack of cash. One hundred thousand American dollars.

I stare at the photo and try to replay what I remembered earlier today, but the rest won't come.

"Not much in here," I say.

"What were you hoping for, a bag full of clues?"

"Actually, kind of. Something—anything, that would make sense of all this."

"What about the boy's?"

I pry the backpack out of Chauncey's hands and replace it with his tiger. He sighs, rolls over, and snuggles the tiger up to his chin.

I take the Glock out of the back of my pants. "This was one of the things in his safety deposit box." I pull a pouch out of the backpack and discover six million dollars worth of bearer bonds, photos of a beautiful woman who I assume was his mother, and a baby journal full of musings in a loopy cursive.

I read the first entry.

As I held you in my arms for the first time, you looked up at me with your big, beautiful eyes. I feel so blessed and fortunate to have you that I decided to name you Chauncey, which means fortune and gamble. We took a gamble by bringing you into this world, but sometimes love trumps good judgment. Your father's job means that even now, as you are born, we are in constant danger. But your father promised to do only one final job, then we will move away and live a happy life together. You, Chauncey, were my gamble, and you are my fortune. And I know that God will bless you with intelligence and a heart full of love.

Sleep well, my beautiful baby boy.

I close the book, not wanting to read anymore of her private thoughts. Intrepid brushes tears off my cheek, tears I wasn't even aware had fallen.

"The world is saying The Priest is dead. What say you?"

"You sound like a pirate." I laugh.

He laughs too.

"He should have gotten out. But if he had, he would have come for his son."

"What happened?"

I tell him about the men who came and all that went down.

"Sounds like the same mercenaries that were at the bank."

"Unless they were Russians."

He tells me about the base takeover in Tartus. That maybe someone is trying to push us toward World War Three.

It all just makes my head hurt.

JUST BEFORE LANDING in London, I'm given a military uniform to change into, so I am not recognized. The boy is taken off the plane inside a large duffle.

Once we get loaded in the armored Range Rover, Intrepid unzips the duffle, and Chauncey pops his little head out and goes, "That was fun!"

We are driven to Notting Hill and let out at a side entrance, where we are greeted by Lorenzo and the smell of bacon cooking, even though it's after two in the morning.

Lorenzo pulls me into his arms and hugs me tightly. Since I'm carrying the boy, he's hugging him too.

He smiles and says, "I'm Chauncey."

"And I'm Lorenzo." He shakes the boy's hand.

"Chauncey," I say. "Lorenzo is the King who granted my knighthood."

The boy's eyes get big as saucers. "Really?"

"Yes, he is." I tell Lorenzo how Chauncey was very brave and how he saved my life. "I think he deserves to be a knight, too."

Lorenzo takes the boy out of my arms and sets him down. "Being a knight is a great responsibility. Are you up for the challenge?"

"I am." Chauncey nods seriously.

Lorenzo holds out one hand for the boy to take and the other for me to take. "Let's go into my study."

When we get into the richly decorated room, Lorenzo grabs a staff out of an umbrella stand and positions the boy in front of him.

Chauncey's eyes are wide with astonishment. He's adorable.

"Wait here," Lorenzo says, then comes back a few moments later wearing his royal dress uniform and looking like the king he is.

"Woah," Chauncey says. "You really are a king."

Lorenzo smiles at him. "Please kneel."

The boy takes the position. He clearly knows the drill.

"A true knight is a man who shows courage and

bravery against all odds. You have proven your valor today, and it is my honor to offer you knighthood. You must promise to uphold the knight's code. Knights are honest, true, and valiant. They must always seek justice and truth. They are noble, chivalrous, and generous. Do you promise to uphold these values?"

"I will," he says.

Lorenzo taps the staff on the boy's right shoulder, then gently raises the staff just up over his head and then taps his left shoulder. "With the power vested to me by country and crown, I make ye a knight of Montrovia."

The boy stands up beaming.

Lorenzo bows to him. "I offer you this staff."

"I get to keep it?"

"Yes, you do. Is Sir Chauncey hungry? I smell bacon."

The boy rubs his tummy. "I smell bacon too. Let's go!"

AFTER A VERY early morning breakfast, we tuck Chauncey in.

"I'm not tired yet," he protests. "Can you tell me a story?"

Lorenzo sits on the edge of the bed and proceeds to make up a story about knights and fair maidens. It's not long before the boy is fast asleep.

Lorenzo takes my hand and leads me into his suite.

"A bed has never felt as soft as this one has," I say, sprawling myself across it, desperately needing sleep.

"You are very upset, Huntley, even though you are putting on a brave face for the boy. Tell me what is going on."

"Can we talk about it after I sleep? I haven't slept in . . . I don't even know how long."

"Well, sleep will have to wait a few more minutes. I need some answers."

"Very well," I say, sitting back up. "Chauncey is the son of the assassin who killed my mother."

"What!? How could that be? Why is he with you?"

"It's a long, crazy story. Let me start at the beginning. Ari and I were sent to the location of the assassin's next hit. Our job was to find him and follow him. We had no idea he was going to shoot Clarice until she walked out of the building—then it was too late. She was shot. Ari went to her and I went after the assassin. Did she make it?"

Lorenzo shakes his head.

"I'm so sorry."

"I spoke with your brother. He filled me in on all that happened to that point. What I want to know is if you kidnapped his son."

My eyes get huge. "No! I would never do something like that!"

"Then tell me the rest."

"Long story short, I followed the man home. I had him on his knees in his living room in the same position he had my mother in. Then the boy spoke from behind me. I didn't know he was there. The assassin begged me not to kill him in front of his son. It was then that I told him about what he did to my mother. He told me that he didn't know I was there. That he was just doing his job. And now, more than ever, I understand. He was given a job, and he did it. Just like I was given the job to kill him. I was trained to complete my missions at all cost. To never question my orders."

"But you are?"

"Yes. Even before his son spoke, I knew I couldn't kill him in cold blood."

"Huntley, you're not a machine," Lorenzo says, joining me on the bed. "You have emotions and feelings, no matter what you were trained for. But if you didn't kill him, why is the American government reporting that the President's assassin is dead?"

"Because that's what I told them."

"Are you saying you lied to your government?"

"I don't know. He may have died in the explosion." I quickly explain the rest of what went down.

"Do you think he could have gotten away?"

"I don't know why he didn't. He was supposed to be right behind us."

"So as far as Black X is concerned, you completed

your mission. Can't you just quit now? Tell them you got the revenge that you wanted, and you are finished. Then you can come live in Montrovia with me. Have a simple life."

"Growing up, we were constantly on the move. I never really had a friend."

"You have me now," he says, pulling me into his arms.

"I know, and it means more to me than you know. But I can't quit. Honestly, I don't think they will let me."

I tell him about Josh and my school.

"I can keep you safe in Montrovia," he suggests.

"I appreciate the offer, Lorenzo, but you can't even keep yourself safe. And there's more going on here. More to the story. I'm starting to believe that my training and missions are somehow connected to my mother's death, and I have to figure out how—with or without the help of Black X."

"Then what?"

"I retire. To your country. If you'll still have me at that point."

"You will be welcomed with open arms, Contessa. Always."

I put my head on his shoulder with a contented sigh and quickly fall to sleep.

MISSION: COMPLETE

I AM AWAKENED by Chauncey, who is riding atop Lorenzo's shoulders. "Time to get up, sleepyhead!"

I glance at the clock by the bed and see that it's nearly noon.

"We're going to play with bubbles!"

"I need a shower."

"He said you would say that." Chauncey laughs out loud. "We're going to the park."

I squint my eyes at Lorenzo.

"It's a large private courtyard," he states. "We'll be perfectly safe."

I smile as the boy pats Lorenzo's shoulders and says, "Giddy up, horsey," causing Lorenzo to rear up and trot around the room.

"Have a good shower," he tells me. "I had clothes

and personal items delivered for you and the boy this morning. Yours are in my closet."

"Thank you," I say gratefully.

He gallops over and kisses me. Then he licks up the side of my cheek, which causes Chauncey to giggle. "That's a horsey kiss!"

AFTER I SHOWER and dress, I meet them in the courtyard.

"Is Daddy still on a trip?" Chauncey asks.

"Yeah, he is," I reply. He nods and then dips the wand back in the bottle and blows more bubbles into the air. I take a seat on the bench next to Lorenzo.

"We're going to have to tell him the truth eventually," he says.

"I know. I guess I just haven't given up hope that he's alive. That he will come find me."

"You hope he's still alive?"

I glance at the boy, who is running around in circles and giggling, trying to catch the bubbles. "For his sake, I do."

Lorenzo tilts his head and studies me. "And what about for your sake?"

I nervously twist my hands together. "I hope so even more."

"The boy adores you," he says, taking my hand in his.

"The boy adores *you*," I counter. "It warms my heart to see how he has taken to you, and how sweet you are to him. You have no idea how much it means to me that you allowed me to bring him here."

"I will do anything you ask of me, because I adore you." He smiles at the boy. "And I will admit, I like the kid. He's smart as a whip and cute as a button. And he already knows how to work it. You should have seen him his morning, sticking out his lower lip in a pout and giving the cook these big, sad eyes because she told him he couldn't have another brownie."

"I take it he got one?"

"Oh, yeah. Got me one an extra one, too," he laughs and rubs his taut belly.

"I promised his father I would keep him safe. I'm not exactly sure how I'm going to do that."

"Gallagher and I have already taken care of it. We've deposited half of the bearer bonds in London and the other half in Montrovia, and a trust has been set up. The boy will live here with a nanny who is an MI5 agent until his father's fate is determined. He met with the nanny this morning, and they are already best friends. I'm leaving four of my father's guards for extra protection, and the house is fully staffed. Gallagher messengered over British citizenship documents for the boy, and he will start school at the prestigious Wetherly Pre-Prep here in Notting Hill. I suggested taking the boy to Montrovia, but Gallagher didn't think it wise."

I cover my face, overcome with emotion.

"Lee," Lorenzo says, kissing me. "Both Gallagher and I can see how attached you are to the boy. And we fully understand why you feel that bond. We know what you, yourself, went through, and we know you want the boy to grow up differently, with or without his father."

"I can't thank you enough."

"Not to mention the fact that he saved your life. For that I will be eternally grateful." He grins at me and grabs my hand. "Come on, let's go play with the bubbles too."

I GIVE CHAUNCEY and Lorenzo hugs and kisses, tell them I will be back in a few days, and then get into a car with William Gallagher.

"I'm coming to Montrovia with you," he says. "Your brother contacted me and requested it."

"Really? Why?"

"I suspect he may have gotten some information from Clarice's home. Have you spoken to him?"

"No. I wasn't sure where he was, and I didn't want anyone to know I was here. The Royal Ascot is in a few days and Lorenzo wants me to accompany him. I told Black X that I would be taking some time off."

"And then you will receive another mission?"

"I assume so. Um, I also just thought of something.

If The Priest is still alive, I think I know why he didn't join us. He might be headed back to America for retribution."

"Should we try to stop him?"

"No," I say, shaking my head. "Because the man he's going after is the guy who ordered the hit on my parents. The former President, John Hillford, Senior. That man double crossed him and tried to have him killed. He wants revenge."

"I don't blame him," he says. "When we get to Montrovia, it will be late. I want you to get a good night's sleep. We'll dig through the clues tomorrow."

"I want to go after the money man."

"The money man?"

"Yes, he's the guy who handled the financial side of things." I mention his name. "Ever heard of him?"

"Oh, yeah. He lives on my turf, and we've been trying to nail him for years."

"I want to find him and work my way up the chain. There's more going on here than a simple assassination. I need to find out what my mom was working on and why she was killed."

"I'll be happy to help you with that endeavor whenever you are ready."

AFTER A QUICK stop in France and an airport change, Intrepid and I officially leave the country as William

Gallagher and Huntley Von Allister.

It's nearly eleven by the time we get to the villa. Ari greets me with a hug and tells me I look tired.

Gallagher repeats what he said about me needing sleep.

I request a glass of wine be brought to my room, then go upstairs, change into a robe, and run a bath.

After the wine is delivered, I slide in the tub and let the warm water soak into my aching body. I call Lorenzo, letting him know that I arrived safely and am going to bed.

When I hang up, I notice today's date on the screen, and realize I can't go to sleep just yet.

AT A FEW minutes before midnight, I sneak down to the kitchen in search of what I need. I find matches on the counter, candles in the pantry, and a cupcake in the refrigerator.

I set the cupcake on the counter, place a single candle in the middle, and light it. Then I place it in my palm, holding it out in front of me.

"Happy Birthday," I say out loud then I close my eyes and make a wish.

"What are you doing?" Ari asks, interrupting me.

"It's just after midnight. The twelfth of June. My birthday."

Ari gets a strange look on his face. "Are you telling

me that today is your actual real life birthday?"

"Yes." I nod. "We didn't get to celebrate our birthdays at school, but I always snuck down at midnight and celebrated like this. I guess it's sort of become my tradition."

"Today is my real life birthday, too," he says.

"Really?"

"Yeah, really."

"Hmm," I say, holding the cupcake between us. "Make a wish, Ari. Then blow out the candle with me."

"One, two, three," he says, both our breaths extinguishing the flame.

"Happy birthday," we say to each other.

"Ari, how old are you?" I ask.

"Well, according to my legend, I'm twenty-one."

"But how old are you, really?"

"I'm now officially nineteen."

I stare at him.

"Why are you looking at me like that?"

"Because I'm turning nineteen today too. How weird is that?"

"It's quite weird, actually." He grabs his phone and types, then reads. "Although nearly nine hundred thousand Americans share the same birthday, only about ten thousand are born on any given date."

"And two of them just happen to be standing here pretending to be brother and sister?"

"We look an awful lot alike," he counters.

"I thought it was good casting."

"Don't you think it's a little odd how comfortable we are with each other? How well we mesh as a team already? How sometimes we don't even have to speak to know what the other is thinking?"

"Good training?" I suggest.

"I'm not attracted to you. You're beautiful, and I am pretty much attracted to anything with a pulse, but—"

"Not me? But you joked about watching my six."

"I was just giving you a hard time—teasing you."

"Are you suggesting that we are really brother and sister, like for real?" I ask.

"Brother and sister? Huntley, if we share the same birthdate and are related, that would make us twins." He stares at me for a beat then says, "What the hell?"

And I have to agree with him.

EPILOGUE

THE LEADER OF Black X sits in a smoke-filled room, enjoying a cigar. He knows he shouldn't smoke inside, but he's celebrating with good reason.

That illusive bastard The Priest is finally really dead.

Something he's been waiting six long years to happen.

"Sir, you're going to want to see this," the Ghost says, interrupting his celebration by throwing a laptop on the desk in front of him and pressing play.

He watches a live feed from the kitchen in the Montrovian villa.

Huntley is alone, standing by the large island with a cupcake in her hand, lighting a single candle at midnight just as she did every year she was at Blackwood.

As she's getting ready to blow it out, Aristotle walks

in on her.

They quickly discover the truth about their birthdays.

"This is bad, boss. They're going to start digging."

"And what if they do? Huntley's birth certificate shows her mother's real name, Kelley Bond. And Aristotle's adoption papers have been in place since he was born, showing that a Kelley Bonde gave him up. An unfortunate typo that wouldn't be that difficult for them to figure out. But that's the point, right? It's all part of their cover. Brother and sister, illegitimate children of Ares Von Allister. Now reunited."

"You and I both know that's not true. Kelley never would have given up her son willingly. When you told her he died shortly after birth, she was heartbroken."

"We had to give the boy to the General. It was the only way to get him to comply. Besides, she got Huntley. She couldn't have handled them both with her career."

"It was cruel."

"It was necessary."

"Do you think all this manipulation is worth it?"

"If we don't fight, who will?"

"You're obsessed with revenge."

He takes a puff of his cigar. "Yes, I am. And I vow to achieve it."

"Have you gotten any updates on her mental state? The old man said she went off grid. Do you know where she went?"

"She killed her mother's assassin. I would assume she felt the need to celebrate."

"And now what? She's accomplished her goal. What if she wants to quit?"

"We can't let that happen."

"Maybe it's time you tell her the truth."

"She and Ari will figure it out in due time. They are curious by nature."

"They are young adults living a dream life in the lap of luxury. There is no reason for them to continue our fight."

"If they want to continue living in the lap of luxury, they must. I suspect her focus will now shift to a higher goal. The Priest and X share many qualities, and we made sure she studied his work extensively as part of her curriculum. I'm told she had great admiration for the man. I was a bit worried that she wouldn't go through with it when the time came. I'm even more in awe of her abilities."

"The old man did a good job training her. You should give him some credit for that."

"She had innate gifts."

"Just like her mother," the Ghost agrees.

The leader picks up his glass and raises it into the air. "May she rest in peace."

The Ghost nods solemnly. "So what's next?"

"Some well-deserved time off, during which I suspect she will realize this is not over. Killing The Priest may have felt like retribution, but I expect the vengeance will feel empty once she realizes he was only the paid trigger man."

"You think she'll do the rest on her own?"

"If not, we'll make it her mission."

ABOUT THE AUTHOR

Jillian is a *USA TODAY* bestselling author. She writes fun romances with characters her readers fall in love with, from the boy next door in the *That Boy* trilogy to the daughter of a famous actress in *The Keatyn Chronicles* series.

She's married to her college sweetheart, has two adult children, two Labs named Cali and Camber, and lives in a small Florida beach town. When she's not working, she likes to decorate, paint, doodle, shop for shoes, watch football, and go to the beach.

www.jilliandodd.net